HAWAII TIME

A PARADISE CRIME COZY MYSTERY
BOOK 3

TOBY NEAL

PARADISE CRIME COZY MYSTERY 3

HAWAII TIME
A Paradise Crime Cozy Mystery
By Toby Neal

BECAUSE CATS...

"In ancient times cats were worshipped as gods; they have not forgotten this."
— Terry Pratchett

1

THE "WITCHING HOUR" at the Ohia Post Office on Maui was the period from three to four p.m. All the folks on the waiting list for boxes remembered that we closed soon and showed up at once to collect their general delivery mail.

"Kat, I've been on the list for a postal box for six years," a youngish woman with a sleeve tattoo and purple hair told me. Her hibiscus print aloha shirt sported a brass name tag over the left boob that reminded me her name was Leona and she worked at the Hotel Hana. "When is someone going to die so I can get my own box?"

I chuckled—but the truth was, people had been dropping like ripe guavas in our tiny village due to a rash of murders, so it wasn't that funny. "I'll see what I can do, Leona. What was your last name again?"

"Baxter."

"Gotcha." I pulled her mail from a folder in a stack of temporary sorting files. She also had a package from an online retailer.

"Seriously. Can you check on the status of my box?" This lady wasn't giving up.

I chewed my bottom lip. "I'll have to get in touch with my boss in Kahului. Can you step aside so I can wait on the rest of the customers?"

"Don't you have a clipboard somewhere?" Leona didn't budge. "I bet Pua knew exactly where I was in the waitlist."

Ugh. Pua Chang. The former postal employee was out on bail, and still a thorn in my side.

"I'm sorry. As you may have noticed, I've been in this job less than a month and I have no help out here. If you could be patient .. ."

"Patient! That's what I've been for SIX YEARS, Kat!" Leona's voice rose. "And now we've got a newbie postmaster who doesn't know her butt from her elbow. Have you lost my application?"

Sometimes it came in handy to be a six-foot-one Secret Service agent temporarily assigned as postmaster: we were trained in crowd control and using body language to convey authority. I straightened to my full height and looked down at Leona Baxter, speaking to her clearly. "Is this what's known as 'going postal' Ms. Baxter? You're having a conniption fit about a structural and institutional shortage, and that isn't going to speed up a solution."

"But we like this line fo' speed up," said the customer behind Ms. Baxter—a rotund, deeply tanned man with a bald pate wearing a rust-colored Primo Beer shirt. "No make *pilikia*, Leona. We all gotta take our turn, and you stay makin' da rest of us wait plenny kine." The customers behind him murmured in support of this—a long line had formed.

"Humph," Leona Baxter said, and stomped out with her package and mail. I had only seen that particular expression in writing before, but that's what she said—"Humph!" Over her shoulder she yelled, "I'm calling the main office in Kahului to complain!"

"You do that," I shot back. "Ask for my supervisor, Mr. Hanoi. I'm sure he'll do what he can to make extra mailboxes appear out of thin air."

I forced a smile as my elderly defender stepped up to the

counter and she disappeared out the glass door. "Here for your mail, Mr. Costa?"

"Yep. Geev'um, Kat," Mr. Costa said.

"What's geev'um?" I fetched his general delivery mail. "I'm still new to the Hawaiian Creole English."

He laughed. "Local kine pidgin, you mean. Geev'um means get after it, go for it. You gonna win. Li'dat."

"Okay. And out of curiosity, Mr. Costa—how long have you been waiting for a box?"

He scratched the white whiskers on his chin. "Mo'bettah, you ask how long I've been in Ohia. Cuz I wen' forget." He chuckled, took his mail, and left as I went on to the next customer.

I was getting better at this job, but the truth was I'd been thrown out here in this tiny village on the "backside" of Maui with little training. In addition, I'd been up to my eyeballs in crime solving while dealing with the former clerk's pristine reputation, even though she'd engaged in criminal activities on behalf of her notorious mob family. My life had been one long bout of whack-a-mole since I arrived in Ohia. The finer points of how the post office was running was the last thing I'd been thinking about.

Closing time rolled around at last. I said goodbye to the final customer of the day, flipping up the old-fashioned counter and following Mrs. Lagustino and her three grandchildren in their Radio Flyer wagon to the glass exit. As I held the door open for them, a tall, slim, outrageously beautiful woman with close-cropped black hair and skin the color of melted bronze walked up. "Kat. It's been a while."

"Sophie!" I dropped my ring of keys in astonishment. "What brings you all the way out here?"

"Helping you with a big problem you've got." Sophie Smithson was a computer wizard and the CEO of a top security firm with offices in Honolulu, Beijing, and Thailand. She was also the daughter of Ambassador Frank Smithson, one of my favorite former protectees during my career in the Secret Service. "I thought I'd better talk with you in person."

"Heck yeah. Get in here, girl." I swung the door wider. "This I've got to hear, even if it's about a big problem."

"It involves your friend Edith Pepperwhite."

My stomach tightened and I realized how empty it was. Had I eaten today? I couldn't remember. "Can we get some food? I need a little fuel for this conversation."

"Indeed," Sophie said. "And we need a quiet place to sit."

"Then let me show you my shack. You'll be surprised when you see it." Of that, I had no doubt. My humble abode out behind the post office still surprised me every day—and not in a good way. I had several "pets" who called it home: first, a large and unpredictably violent cat named Tiki; second, a giant cane spider named Miss Prissy who lived in my shower; and last but not least, a pair of geckos named Tweedledum and Tweedledee who hung out over the stove waiting for stray bugs.

Sophie's eyebrows went up. She looked like Nefertiti the Egyptian queen with a question on her mind. "This I have to see."

I ushered her inside, locked the outer doors, and showed her the premises with pride. "I haven't been here long, but the post office is the hub of Ohia."

Sophie smiled. "I'm happy to see you've landed on your feet in this unexpected posting, though I can't help but think it's a sad waste of your many talents. You were an exceptional Secret Service agent."

I shrugged, suppressing a twinge of grief. I'd put everything I had into my career, only to end up here, far away from a handsy Congressman with way too much power. I'd recently declined an opportunity to leave for a dream detail in the White House. "And I will be again, someday. But for now, I'm making the most of my time in paradise. Come on back and see my shack. You're going to love the palm tree growing out of the rain gutter!"

2

ANA:

The bad thing with getting revenge is that sometimes it doesn't go as planned and can even bite you in the tush—my situation, for instance.

I hate my grandma and tried to gun her down on the steps of a courthouse on Oahu, for good reasons. Getting back at her for being such a self-righteous hypocrite and ensuring my mom's inheritance of her estate should not have become as messy and complicated as it ended up. I was being chased not only by cops, but also by the FBI.

"That mean old bag," I muttered, squeezing the steering wheel of my stolen rust bucket Toyota Corolla as if it were Edith Pepperwhite's scrawny neck. "I can't believe she sold me out and turned me in with that list of charges."

"Well, you did try to shoot her, sweetie." Mom, beside me, clutched the armrest as we drove high into the hills above Honolulu. "Eyes on the road, Ana. My mother will get what she deserves when we're through with her."

Mom shared my grandma's short stature and stocky build, though the blonde hair touching her shoulders came from a bottle and my grandma's was pure white with age. Thankfully, I got lucky in the looks department, because the two of them looked like lady lawn gnomes.

Good looks came to me from the man in my family tree, though he didn't stick around beyond the impregnation stage. He's on my revenge list, too. It's a long list, but I thought I'd start with the low-hanging fruit. Turns out sometimes they can be the toughest.

"I'm expressing myself. You told me I shouldn't bottle things up inside." I glanced sideways at Mom.

"But really. What were you thinking, Ana?" Mom grumped. "You should've known going after Edith in public would bring some serious heat."

"Mom! Quit harping on me." I cranked a turn hard enough to throw her against the door. "You wanted me to deal with her permanently, and I was disguised. No one can say for sure I was the one shooting at her."

"I know, but they suspect you, and with the list of things you did, you're a wanted woman. I'm worried."

I blew out a breath that lifted the bangs on my forehead. Mom fussing was one more hassle I had to deal with. "You're Edith's heir, Mom. When she's gone, we'll get that cute little house in Hana and the fortune Edith's got squirreled away where I couldn't get to it— all those stocks, bonds, and whatnot." I frowned. What an opportunity I'd lost when that giant of a woman protecting Edith got her out of range of my gun. "If Ralph and I had succeeded in shooting her, I'd have stopped her from filing a cease and desist on the development at New Ohia. The plan was perfect."

"Except it didn't work." Mom folded her arms over her chest and pushed out her lip.

"Yeah, well, who knew Edith had that Amazon guarding her? What am I supposed to be, psychic?" Nothing I did made Mom happy. "Anyway, at least I'm done with Ralph. What a waste of time he was."

"Men are always a waste of time."

Not always. Even Ralph had been fun in the sack, but I wasn't going to waste words trying to convince Mom a good shag was worth some inconvenience. "We're starting fresh. And we've got new friends in high places who want to help."

Mom frowned. "What are you up to, now?"

I lost it. "Mom! I told you! We're going to the Changs. Why do you think we're driving up this ridiculous mountain?" Off to one side, the ocean seemed a long way down.

"That could be risky. Why would they help us?"

"You told me to take care of Edith, and then you didn't like the way I tried to do it. I've had enough of your attitude." I pulled the car over onto the narrow shoulder above a cliff. We were ascending into one of those fancy neighborhoods above Honolulu, the kind of place I'd never been able to afford. Nor had Mom. After Edith gave Mom up for adoption and her family fell apart early on, she'd ended up in foster care. She'd had me when she was seventeen because . . . well, who knows? But the school of hard knocks made me harder and smarter. Not Mom. She wanted things to be handed to her because she stuck out her lip out and pouted. "Get out of the car. I've got no room for whiners."

Mom blinked her big blue eyes at me. They were her best feature. "You're going to drop your mother off on the side of the road, on a mountain, no less?"

"Yep. Either you're in all the way, or you're out. What's it going to be?"

Mom was in. I was stuck with a sidekick toting more personal baggage than a 747, and few skills to make the hassle of dealing with her worthwhile.

Once we were on the road again, Mom pulled out a little silver flask and took a sip. "You're a tough cookie, Ana."

"I know." I was playing a long game. My eyes were on a prize on the other side of Mom. She was a speed bump in the road on my way to a better life.

3

I LOCKED the back door of the post office and pointed Sophie toward the weather-beaten, one-room dwelling behind the main building. An unpaved parking lot surrounded us, with the general store on one side. That open, potholed space butted up against a patch of hibiscus and ginger that girded one side of the shack. A rickety porch with a rail defined the front, and an open area of tussocky grass segued into a wall of green jungle behind it.

"This is where I live," I said. "It's assigned lodging for post office staff. I can't decide what I like about it more—the beach rock front step or the palm tree growing out of the roof's gutter." We both eyed my abode with our hands on our hips.

"Unfortunately, you're going to have to transplant that coconut palm soon," Sophie said in her plummy accent. "So I'd choose the beach rock as a personal favorite."

"You're right, of course." I'd forgotten how literal Sophie was. "And that cat on the porch is Tiki. Do not approach her; she's feral."

"Feral in what way?" Sophie cocked her head, eyeing the massive calico. Tiki eyed her right back, flattening her only remaining ear and lashing her kinked tail.

"Tiki's a stray that does whatever she wants, including clawing at humans. She came with the shack. I had no say in it."

"Ah. Well, your place seems a bit small for visiting, and the feline appears unfriendly. Why don't we go to my lodgings, the Hotel Hana, and I'll treat you to drinks and a meal?"

Of course Sophie was staying at the most expensive place in Hana. Money had never been an issue for her or her family. "Fabulous. I'll change and feed Tiki, then we can go."

"I'll be in the car." Sophie indicated a white Ford SUV marked with a Security Solutions logo parked beside the post office.

"Your business keeps a car here on Maui?"

"We have several. Security Solutions has a good number of cases on the island, and it's saved money in the long run as well as being more convenient for our operatives."

"I didn't realize." I ogled the SUV longingly. I'd been doing without a set of wheels since I made the move to Ohia and being without a car had become a real pain in my patootie.

"Many of our best clients are celebrities. Maui seems to be a favorite hideout for them since it has a 'do not approach' county ordinance that protects their dwellings."

"You'll have to tell me more about that over dinner. Give me a few minutes to freshen up, and I'll be right there."

I sidled past Tiki, murmuring soothing nonsense, and fumbled through my keys to unlock the front door.

Across the parking lot, Opal and her husband Artie exited the main door of their business, the Ohia General Store. She swept the porch while the slack-key musician settled with his guitar in his favorite wooden chair on the *lanai*.

"Who's your friend?" Opal hollered across the parking lot.

Opal Pahinui was neither shy nor quiet. A naturally curious person with a psychic gift for reading runes, she and her Hawaiian husband had been in Ohia for almost thirty years. They were at the heart of the area's "coconut wireless" gossip circuit, and fast becoming a second family to me. Today, Opal wore a tie-dyed scarf around her shoulders held in place with a rhinestone pin that dazzled in the late afternoon sun.

"I'll bring her over to meet you," I yelled back, knowing that nothing less would satisfy Opal.

Once inside the shack, I yanked off my sweaty work polo with the brass name badge spelling out KAT SMITH, POSTMASTER. I put the name badge away for the next workday and did a quick splash at the sink with a washcloth. I tugged my long, brown hair out of its ponytail, hung my head upside down, and brushed it vigorously. A swipe of lipstick and a whisk of mascara completed my grooming.

I changed into a scoop neck dark blue tee that Aunt Fae had given me at Christmas last year, saying "the color matches your eyes." Adding a cup of kibble to Tiki's bowl, I was ready to go.

Sophie obliged my request that she come meet Opal and Artie. Together we picked our way around the perpetual puddles of the parking lot toward the sagging wooden porch of the store.

"Oh my, Artie. I wish you could see these young ladies coming toward us," Opal said, squeezing her blind husband's shoulder. "They are both so beautiful."

"Um, thanks?" I'd never been great at compliments, especially about my looks. I could tell by Sophie's strained smile that she didn't love them either. Tell me I was smart or strong, though, and I was putty in your hands. "Artie, Opal, this is my friend Sophie Smithson. She's the CEO of a security firm and the best computer expert I know. Her ambassador father was one of my favorite protectees when I was in the Secret Service."

"Delighted to meet you," Sophie said, shaking hands with Opal, then Artie.

Artie held Sophie's long, tawny fingers in his big hands. His sightless eyes seemed to stare right into a person's soul, and he radiated a calm dignity that always made me wish I had more time to spend with him. A large man, he wore baggy Bermuda shorts with an aloha shirt and compression stockings on his legs. "You've been through a long, deadly hurricane in your life," he said slowly.

Sophie went still, gazing at Artie intently. "Yes. I have been through a personal hurricane."

"Better times are coming for you," Artie said.

"I sincerely hope so." Tears sprang into Sophie's big brown eyes. "It's been challenging."

Artie patted the hand he clasped and released her at last. "You'll be fine. The worst is over. Peace is on its way."

"Peace would be lovely," Sophie said.

Opal wasn't the only one with a psychic gift. Artie had one too, of a different kind.

We made conversation for a few minutes, then said our good-byes when a carload of tourists pulled up and parked their minivan at the store.

Sophie got behind the wheel but was quiet as we drove toward Hana on the narrow, two-lane road. "Your friends are remarkable," she said at last.

"I think so, too. They're part of the reason I've decided to stay in Ohia longer. My boss Ben wanted to transfer me, but I said no. They're *'ohana*, as they say in Hawaii." I was pleased to use a Hawaiian word I'd learned recently. "Family."

Sophie glanced at me. "That is the best kind."

"I don't have any relatives other than Aunt Fae back in Maine, so that's the kind that matters to me. Speaking of family, how is the Ambassador? Frank?" Francis Smithson had been the finest man I'd had the privilege of guarding. He'd always insisted I call him by his first name.

"Dad's fully retired now. He recovered well from the gunshot incident with my mother, but he's still fighting cancer. He's doing well, all things considered."

Talk about a dysfunctional family—Sophie had that in spades. Her parents had taken the phrase "bad divorce" to new levels.

"I'm sorry I forgot about his cancer in all the craziness. I meant to call him, but there's no signal in my shack and when I'm at the post office, it's busy all the time."

"Tell me about what's been going on. Other than a phone call or two when you first reached out to me, I don't have the full picture of what's been happening out here." Sophie took a hairpin turn with aplomb, dodging a chicken pecking at a fallen mango on the road.

"First, I want to know what brought you all the way here so unexpectedly," I said. "It's not every day I get a visitor in Ohia. In fact, you're my first one."

"And I wish it was a purely social call, but to be fair, I had other business on Maui, too." Sophie navigated one of the sharp turns hung about with dangling tropical vines. "Let's wait for this conversation until we're settled and have a drink in front of us."

"Works for me," I said. "As long as it's not a Blue Hawaiian."

Sophie chuckled. "I'll have one for both of us." She was the only person I knew who liked that luridly colored, sweet, frothy abomination. "Have you met anyone interesting out here?" She quirked a brow. "Rumor has it you're dating a pilot."

"I don't do relationships," I said. "But I do have a special friend who flies for a small local airline and built his own airplane. His name is Mr. K, and I'll save talking about him for drinks, too."

4

ANA:

The mansion we'd reached was perched near the top of a mountain overlooking Honolulu. Inside, I perched on a leather couch so big and so white it hurt my eyeballs. Mom, clutching her knockoff Louis Vuitton bag nervously, plopped down beside me.

The couch was too soft, and Mom was too close. She slid into me as I fell into her. We floundered like a couple of puppies on a beanbag. It wasn't a good look with a gangster watching us from across the room.

Finally, with a muttered curse, I pushed Mom out of my lap and positioned her a couple feet away, handing her the giant purse. It was heavy enough to have a bowling ball inside. She was probably packing her gold-plated pistol, the only thing of value she'd kept from her last divorce. The guards had frisked us, but they hadn't bothered with Mom's bag, the fools.

But Fabio Chang didn't look like a fool. The son of an Italian model and the grandson of infamous Healani Chang from the crime family that dominated the Big Island of Hawaii, he sprawled with his arms spread along the back of an identical loveseat facing ours. Straight, long, bleached blond hair framed a handsome face with a sexy, ruthless mouth. A white shirt was open at his neck, revealing a muscular golden chest. He would have seemed like an anime character if his eyes hadn't been so cold.

"Are you comfortable, ladies?" His tone was lightly ironic.

"Finally, we are. Yes," I said. "Thanks for meeting with us."

"I hear you have information about our situation in Ohia."

"I do," I said.

"We do," Mom said.

We spoke at the same time.

I held up a hand, palm facing her. "Let me do the talking, Mom."

She folded her arms over her middle and pushed out her lip.

I turned to face Chang. "You're different than I expected." I caught his eyes with mine, then fluttered my lashes. I leaned forward so my arms pushed my chest out, displaying my assets. "More handsome."

He did not reply.

"Great place you have here." I gazed through a pair of glass sliders at the ocean. The silhouette of Diamond Head was visible in the distance; this was why rich people built in the mountains above Honolulu. "A stunning view. Worthy of your family name. As is the development in New Ohia." I uncrossed and recrossed my legs in the miniskirt Mom said was too short for a business meeting and glanced up. "I have a proposition."

"Is that so?" Chang's expression hadn't changed, but his eyes had narrowed. He'd noticed my antics.

"I do. Yes." I breathed the last word as if whispering in his ear.

"Go on." He removed his arms from the back of the couch and leaned toward me.

"I'll trade what I know about the players opposing New Ohia for your help in getting rid of them, beginning with one old woman who shouldn't be much of a challenge. Her name is Edith Pepper-white, Esquire."

Beside me, Mom stiffened slightly, which upset our delicate balance. She tipped toward me. I shoved her back upright.

"I know the name," Chang said. "That lawyer's been a problem."

"She's been a problem for us, too. And if she was gone, the lawsuit against your development in New Ohia would lose focus and momentum. It would also send a message to anyone opposing it."

"The FBI is involved," he said. "Too late for that."

"Dead women tell no tales. To law enforcement, or anyone for that matter."

Chang stared at me for another long minute, then stood abruptly. I wouldn't be able to get up from this cursed couch with a fraction of the animalistic grace he showed as he stalked over to a wet bar against the mirrored wall and opened the cabinet doors. "Drink?"

"Yes, please," Mom said. "Bourbon. Make it a double."

"Sparkling water for me," I said.

A moment later, Chang handed Mom an amber-filled tumbler tinkling with ice, which she gulped.

He handed me a crystal glass filled with bubbling water, our fingers brushing and sending a zing through me that lit my body up.

"Would you like to see the view from the top floor?" he asked. His slithery dark gaze wandered over me.

I shivered deliciously. "Yes, please."

Mom wallowed, preparing to rise. He gently pushed her back. "Why don't you rest. Enjoy your drink and help yourself to the wet bar if you need a refill." Chang had Mom's number, all right.

Mine too, it turns out, as he took my hand and tugged me to my feet, sparing me a fight with the upholstery and letting me feel his strength. "Right this way, beautiful. You'll enjoy this."

I was sure I would—and the murder we'd plan afterward, too.

5

Once Sophie and I were seated in the Hotel Hana's restaurant, near an open window where we could look out over the lush grounds, I raised my drink. I liked a good quality Scotch on the rocks, nothing frou-frou, always the same no matter where in the world the bar was. "To old friends and new adventures."

"Indeed." Sophie lifted her bright blue, pineapple and umbrella decorated monstrosity. We clinked glasses and sipped.

I gazed around an open-air setting overlooking landscaping of mature tropical trees with the ocean in the distance. The single malt lit a warm path down my throat and hit my stomach like a tiny grenade. "Whew. I need to get some food onboard quick. It was a long day, and I can't remember when I ate last."

"I'm just in time, then." A server with a plumeria barrette holding back rippling black hair set a native wood platter loaded with fragrant bread in front of us. A pat of butter in the shape of a shell, enhanced by a fresh orchid, invited demolishment. "Are you Kat? The postmaster?"

"I am." I squinted to read her name badge. "Hello, Lani. I'm working on memorizing all of our general delivery folks, but I don't think I've seen you before."

She smiled. "That's because I'm one of the lucky ones. I share a box with the Nakasone family."

I suppressed a wince. Sandy and Windy Nakasone, two mother-less girls in Ohia, were the bane of my existence. Each day when they showed up to check their box, they showered me with sass. "Ah. I've seen your name with theirs. Are you their aunt?"

"Yes. The girls have been upset about Auntie Pua's departure from the post office. She was a big support to them." Lani turned to Sophie. "I'm so sorry to talk shop while you're having dinner. Let me make it up to you both with another round of drinks."

"Oh, no. Please do go on," Sophie smiled. "I'm delighted to have a peek into Kat's new life."

Lani smiled at me apologetically. "My brother and I are sorry they've been such terrors. I'm living with them in Ohia since his wife's passing, and we do what we can, but we both have to work. They're on their own a lot and they haven't gotten over their mama's death."

"Oh, I understand." I had already looked into what could be done to curb the girls' lack of supervision. No services were avail-able in our remote location, and the family's finances didn't seem to support paid caregivers; but even if such things had been available I'd been told in no uncertain terms to mind my own business. The community was looking after the girls as best they could. "I am trying to build rapport with them, but it's tough going."

"Tell me about it." Lani rolled her eyes. "Those girls can be real *titas*."

"What's a *tita*?" Sophie asked.

"A pidgin word for . . . a strong-minded female?" I said.

Lani laughed. "It's more than that. *Titas* are loyal to a fault, speak their mind, and aren't afraid to back their mouths up with fists."

"Perfect. I understand now." I made a little bow.

"Anyway, if they give you a hard time, drop me a note in the box. They won't open anything addressed to me. At least, I don't think so." Lani rolled her eyes. "I told them opening other people's mail is a federal offense."

"It is, and thanks for that offer. Is there anything else I can do to make up for not being Auntie Pua?"

"Candy in the box might help. Pua used to slip them treats. But you didn't hear it from me if my brother ever asks." Lani winked before bustling off.

I grabbed a slice of the soft, warm bread and buttered it generously. "I feel sorry for them, but those girls are naughty. I'm not sure candy is the way to go."

Sophie pursed her lips around her straw and gave a long pull on her fluorescent blue drink. "Sometimes you have to soothe with food. That cat of yours, for instance."

"Tiki is a menace, too, but you're right. Dinner scraps and kibble have been a big part of improving our relationship." I started on my second hunk of bread. "I'm thrilled we recently got over the flea bath hurdle." After another delicious bite I pointed my butter knife at Sophie. "Quit the suspense and tell me why you came all the way out to Ohia."

"I had to travel to Maui for a Security Solutions case, so it's not entirely your fault I'm on the island," Sophie said in her pedantic way. "Remember you asked me to do a deep dive into the online activity behind New Ohia?"

"Dimly. That seems like ages ago." In fact, it had only been a week since my last impromptu investigation wrapped with a couple of arrests and the news that the big, fancy new development called New Ohia next to our little town was now under a court ordered cease and desist, pending investigation. Edith Pepperwhite had filed those papers to get the development stopped. I'd gone with her to Oahu and ended up protecting her from an attack by her vengeful granddaughter Ana and Ana's misguided boyfriend, Ralph.

It had been a gloriously quiet week recuperating from all that and I wasn't in a hurry to dig it all up again. I sipped my Scotch for courage. "Well, lay it on me."

"Do you mean explain the circumstances which bring me here? 'Lay it on me' sounds like you want me to . . . tell you the facts."

I sometimes forgot Sophie grew up overseas and that English was a second language for her. "Yes. That's what it means."

Just then, a fresh round of drinks arrived via the bartender. Lani had made good on her offer. Finishing my first drink, I felt ready to hear whatever she had to say. "Give it to me straight. Hit me with your best shot. I'm all ears, baby. Shoot from the hip as you bring me up to speed."

Sophie blinked. "Many colloquialisms there. We can address those some other time." She leaned in closer. "What have you heard of the Chang crime family?"

Unfortunately, I'd heard a lot, and none of it was good.

6

I took a bracing belt of my second Scotch and leaned forward. Sophie and I were practically knocking our foreheads together in an effort not to be overheard in the open restaurant. "Tell me what you know about the Changs and their involvement with New Ohia," Sophie said. "After, I'll fill in what I've uncovered."

That seemed sensible. "I'm aware the Chang crime family is involved with New Ohia, if that's what you're going to say," I said. "Pua Chang, who worked at the post office when I arrived, is a member of that family. She told me that she helped organize the New Ohia development and get it off the ground, with a goal of making the place a retreat for family members to return to, because Ohia is the town where the Changs originally got established in Hawaii." My tongue tripped over a word here and there, so I slowed, enunciating with care. "I got ahold of a memory drive with the former development manager's records on it. With the forensic accountant Hermione Leede's help—you gave me her name and number—we uncovered a scam New Ohia Vision was running. They were selling lots that were leased from the state of Hawaii that they had no authority to sell."

"Yes, yes." Sophie flapped a hand and burped. Those two Blue

Hawaiians were having an effect on her as well. "Hopefully the investigation by the FBI brings all that to light in an evil—evid—evid-en-tial way." She hiccupped and reached for her water glass to take a swig. "That's not what I came to talk about."

"Oh yeah?" I took a belt of water, too. Couldn't be a bad idea. "Tell me. At last. Please."

"Ana Davies, Edith Pepperwhite's granddaughter, has gone to the Changs for help. That's my news."

I rocked back in my chair, blinking. "Wha—?"

Lani returned with our entrees, interrupting my ability to process, which was already poor due to imbibing. I hardly remembered ordering the thick, juicy, grass-fed local steak smothered in mushroom and wine sauce, but I sure needed it to counteract the alcohol. I glanced over. Sophie faced a massive, barbecued pork chop topped with a pineapple compote framed in sautéed vegetables. "Let's get some more food in us before we go any further with this."

Sophie nodded. She was already cutting into her dinner.

A good bit of time passed as we stuffed our faces. I hadn't had such a good meal since I went on a date with Mr. K to the nearby steakhouse.

Finally, I sat back from my cleaned plate, dabbing my mouth with a napkin. "How did you find out Ana is talking to the Changs?"

Sophie shrugged. "Do you really want to know the specifics? It involves a top-secret data aggregation program that scrapes the Internet for keywords and can penetrate firewalls and . . ."

"Actually, no. I don't need the specifics. I guess a better question is, how reliable is this information?"

"Very reliable."

"And who in the Chang family has she approached? Not that I'm familiar with them."

"I'm sure the names I uncovered would be known and of interest to law enforcement." Sophie chased the last of her Blue

Hawaiian around the bottom of her glass with the straw, making a loud slurping sound. "I've notified my friend Marcella Scott, The FBI agent working the case."

"That's good. I'm wondering what I, personally, can do about this info."

Lani came by again. "I see you ladies enjoyed your meal. Can I tempt you with a slice of fresh lilikoi cheesecake, or a strawberry guava tart?"

Sophie and I exchanged a glance. "Bring one of each and a couple of forks," I said.

"You're in for a treat," Lani said with a wink, and left with our empty dishes balanced on her arms.

Sophie yawned suddenly. "Apologies. I got up early this morning with the baby, and then the toddler got up too. They're both active children and once they wake up—well, nobody's getting any sleep after that."

"Do you still have that terrific ninja nanny, Armita?" I wasn't the first to call the petite, wiry Thai woman who lived with Sophie and wore nothing but black by that nickname.

"I couldn't make my life work without her," Sophie said. "I heard a term recently—'co-parenting.' That's what Armita and I do. She is so much more than a nanny. She keeps my home going."

"You're lucky to have her."

"I know. She's a second mom, not just to my children, but to me."

Lani reappeared and set down pretty plates, each with an artistically enhanced dessert upon it. "*Lilikoi* is the Hawaiian name for passionfruit, and it has a unique sweet and tart tropical flavor. Strawberry guava is also known as *waiawī*. The fruits are not commercially raised, so it's rare to find them in cuisine. They are part of our farm to table and foraging movement here at the Hotel Hana."

"I've had them before," Sophie said. "They're smaller and sweeter than regular guavas."

"I might have tried one on a hike," I told Sophie. "A reddish fruit a little bigger than a grape?"

"Yes, dark pink on the outside, which is why they're nicknamed 'strawberry,'" Lani said. "Enjoy."

Sophie told Lani to put everything on her room tab.

"So," Sophie said. "Tell me about the pilot you're dating."

"Keone Kaihale. We're . . . um . . ." I fiddled with my fork . . . "friends with occasional entry-level benefits."

"That's a start. What's he like?" Sophie sliced her fork into the fluffy cheesecake drizzled with jonquil yellow syrup. "Marcella tells me women want to talk about all the details of their relationships."

"That's what I hear." I moved the miniature tart with its glazed crust oozing pink juice closer to me. "But there's not much to tell. We hang out. Go surfing. We had one steak dinner. He's nice." I didn't want to jinx what we had going by talking about it.

"No details is fine with me, because I'm the last person you want to talk to about relationships." Sophie shook her head. "Are you going to eat that tart, or can I have some of that one too?"

I broke into the guava tart's sugar-glazed crust and forked a bite into my mouth. "Mmm. This is so good. Kind of reminds me of the strawberry rhubarb pie Aunt Fae would make in the summertime in Maine."

"I'd love to try that someday." Sophie dug into the tart and passed me the cheesecake. We demolished the desserts, and by then, I was feeling closer to sober.

"I love a tasty business meeting," Sophie said with satisfaction, pushing the plate away and dabbing her mouth.

"Even if it's bad news?"

"Even then you're good company. I like getting to know you in a new context," Sophie said. "Before it was always all about your work with my dad."

"Those days feel like a lifetime ago," I said, remembering the days as part of her ambassador father's detail. "But what can we do to protect Edith? I thought she'd be safe with the court papers filed, but if Ana is still coming after her . . ."

"It seems she might be. If Edith doesn't lead the legal movement against New Ohia, the civil lawsuit might lose momentum even with the FBI investigating," Sophie said. "The Changs have good reasons to get her out of the way."

"It's still early—not even dark. What do you say I call Edith? She can come over to the hotel and you can tell her more about this situation. She should be warned directly. Then maybe she can give me a ride home, and you can call it a night."

Sophie yawned again. "That sounds lovely. I'd appreciate being able to head off to bed."

I phoned Edith on my cell and asked her to come meet us. "We need to brainstorm a bit," I told my elderly friend. "It's about your granddaughter."

"Oh dear," Edith said. "I'll get my hat and be there in a jiffy."

But as the minutes ticked by and Edith neither appeared nor answered her phone, I grew more and more anxious. Even the soothing sounds of the fountain in the front lobby of the hotel and the soughing of the wind in the palms couldn't calm my nerves.

Ana Davies was deadly, and the Changs were worse. How much trouble was my friend Edith in?

7

I WAS PACING ANXIOUSLY around the entrance to the hotel while Sophie yawned on a padded bench when Edith rolled up—in the passenger seat of her friend Josie's Volkswagen van.

I'd first met these ladies for the first time at the post office when the local Red Hat Society came over for their monthly "buy all the stamps with women on them" outing. Of course, tonight they were wearing their favorite scarlet chapeaux.

I waited impatiently as Edith hopped down from her seat and Josie waved for a valet to come park the car. Of course they knew the staff, so Sophie and I cooled our heels while they greeted and hugged everyone and "talked story" for a few minutes. This was the protocol whenever locals encountered each other, and anything less was considered rude.

It took a few more minutes for the valet to help Josie with her oxygen canister on its wheeled trolley to the sidewalk. Edith took Josie's arm, and they made their way over to us as he drove the van to the parking lot across the street.

"What happened?" I asked Edith without preamble. "I was worried."

"Kat! My very own Secret Service agent," Edith said. The lawyer was so short that the brim of her witch-style hat only came to my shoulder. "My car's electric, and the battery's dead. Took me a minute to get sorted and call Josie, so we came in her car." She turned to Sophie. "You must be the computer and security whiz Kat told us about."

"Hello. Yes, I'm Sophie Smithson. Pleased to meet you, Edith. And this is?"

"Josie Manahuli." Josie and Sophie shook hands. Josie was as tall as Sophie, around five foot nine. She wore a long, flowered muumuu with a gardenia pinned behind her ear. The blossom spiked the air with fragrance. "Pleased to meet you."

"Likewise. I asked the staff for a quiet spot for us to meet, and they said the library was free. Follow me, please." Sophie led us past the check-in counter and around an open-air fountain whose basin swam with koi, and on to an intimate room. The library was lined with shelves of popular books and equipped with a seating area in one corner.

"Kat thought I should share some information with you first-hand. As she told you, I'm the CEO of a security company."

"It's generous of you to come all this way," Edith said, adjusting her purple tunic.

"I owe Kat a lot. She was my father's protection agent. Anyway, I came across some information regarding your granddaughter that you need to know. Additionally, I have some ideas to help you stay safe during this trying time."

"Stay safe? I thought the crisis on the courthouse steps was the last of it." Edith sat on the loveseat and tugged Josie down beside her, keeping a grip on the other woman's hand. "I'm ready to hear the latest on my granddaughter."

A thought suddenly occurred to me. "Are—are you two a couple?"

Edith peeked almost shyly at Josie from beneath the brim of her hat. "Are we, dear one?"

"Yes, we are," Josie said softly. "It's time people knew it." She lifted the lawyer's hand and kissed Edith's knuckles tenderly, then addressed me. "My husband died five years ago. My children are grown and gone. Life is too short not to love who you love."

I blinked because something got in my eye; surely that was it.

I glanced at Sophie, and she nodded. "That's good. Two are always better than one in a threat situation. You can keep an eye on each other."

"Tell me more about this threat situation," Edith said.

"Sophie found out that Ana has reached out to the Changs for help," I said.

"Help for what?" Edith's brows came together in puzzlement.

"Help in dealing with you," Sophie said gently. "I picked up some texts and phone calls. She's in touch with a branch of the Changs on Oahu. Last message I intercepted indicated they'd set up a meeting."

"Oh." Edith's face had gone pale. She took off her hat and set it beside her on the couch. Her short white hair made her seem small, vulnerable. "I feel a little overheated."

Josie held Edith's hand in both of hers. "Why is this happening? Why would Ana want to hurt you? I don't understand."

"Have you told Josie everything?" I asked Edith. "About Ana?"

Edith shook her head, then shifted on the couch so she could face the other woman. "Josie, I've been so ashamed. Not ashamed of my choice to give Ana's mother up for adoption, but of what happened after my decision to take my granddaughter Ana in last year and try to make it up to her. I told you it didn't work out; I sent her back to Oahu. What I didn't tell you was that Ana stole my passwords and used them to break into my accounts and clean them out. The only thing she didn't get into was my stock and retirement portfolios, which are secure with a financial planner."

Josie's tan complexion went a little green. She inhaled vigorously through her cannula several times. "I'm sad you didn't trust me enough to tell me. I know you said money was tight for a while, but I didn't realize . . ."

"I was able to increase dispersals from my retirement plans and get back on track, but Ana took everything I had on hand," Edith sighed. "My granddaughter said she'd leave without a fuss if I agreed not to tell anyone. I wrote everything up and told her that documentation would go to the police if she did anything further. When she rifled my room on Oahu looking for the cease and desist order for New Ohia, I turned that document in to the police."

"That set her off further, didn't it?" Sophie said. "Because after that she tried to gun you down on the courthouse steps. She seems determined to kill you."

I wished Sophie weren't so brutal with the facts as Edith covered her face with her hands. I patted the older woman's purple-clad knee. I'd come to care for Edith through our shared adventure with the court filing on Oahu.

"I don't think Ana knew Edith turned her in," I said. "She already had her plans in motion with her boyfriend Ralph. Thanks to his warning and Sophie's, we're ahead of Ana and the Changs and can prepare for what's coming." I firmed my jaw. "I'll need to come out to your house, Edith, and help you make it defensible."

Edith lived in Hana in a little plantation cottage with an orchid-filled yard. Fort Knox it was not. We'd have our hands full making it safe. In fact, my brain was boggling a little at the task. "I should come home with you. We don't know when they will make a move."

Edith frowned. "It's fine. Nothing's changed in the last five minutes."

"These are serious people, Edith, and Ana is a little . . ." I tapped my temple. "Unpredictable. You need to take steps."

Edith focused bright blue eyes on Sophie. "You're the CEO of a security firm, yes? How about I hire you?"

Sophie blinked but her expression didn't change. "That would be wise, Ms. Pepperwhite."

"Please, call me Edith. Now get on the phone and get some of your people out to guard me. Let's start there."

"Most of our personnel are already on jobs, and they're not on

Maui. I'll have to work with our dispatch unit to bring the right people around, and none of them are nearby. Let me get on the phone and see what I can set up." She stood and walked away, already on her device.

I glanced back at Edith and Josie. "Let's start by moving you to Josie's house until we can shore up the security at your place. I'll spend the night with you two and bring my weapon. It's a start." I took out my phone. "Now, let's call Lei and Pono and let them know you have a credible threat against your life and you're hiring Sophie's firm."

Edith rolled her eyes but said nothing as I rang the detectives we'd been working with since the first body I'd found in Ohia.

8

EDITH and I rattled along the deserted road to Ohia with Josie at the wheel of the VW. Sophie had bid us goodbye and gone to get some much needed rest in her hotel room. We were on our way to the shack so I could pick up my weapon before going to Josie's house in Ohia, where Edith would spend the night.

"What about Butter?" Edith said. "She's going to expect me to come home."

"Your cat's a sweetie, but she's independent," Josie said. "Besides, you have that automatic food and water dispenser filled up, don't you?"

"I guess so." Edith sat in the seat behind Josie with me in the front passenger seat. I'd put her there as a more secure position in case of attack. Her face was pallid in the light from the dash. The news that her granddaughter was gunning for her, and now had reinforcements, hit her hard. She gripped the armrest of the bench seat tightly as we took a turn a little too fast.

I reviewed the plan we'd come up with at the library. "Tonight, I'll come back to Josie's house with you two and keep watch. Tomorrow, while I'm at work, Sophie will stay with you until her security team from Oahu arrives. Your investment in hiring her firm is a smart one, Edith. The police can't cover all the bases with a situation like this, nor take action until an incident has occurred."

"I understand."

"After the security team arrives, they'll move you to a secret, more secure location until Ana is captured, the investigation into New Ohia is complete, or both. Preferably, both," I said. "I'm sorry this is going to be expensive, but better to be safe than the alternative."

A long silence went by. The van's round headlights picked out the bright yellow eyes of frogs as we clattered along. Overgrown ferns brushed against the van, and bits of moonlit sky showed through trees silhouetted against the velvet night.

"I don't like this plan," Edith said suddenly.

I gritted my teeth. I had been waiting for this.

Edith Pepperwhite was a strong, independent woman who'd lived her life for more than seventy years the way she wanted to, a pioneer for women in her field. Submitting to others' suggestions for her well-being was not going to sit well with her. In fact, I was surprised she'd gone along with our recommendations so far without an objection.

I kept my eyes on the road, watching it unspool in the tropical darkness ahead, as Josie drove the narrow, potholed route to Ohia. "What don't you like about it?"

"I don't like going to another location. I want to stay in my home."

"I understand, but that's not practical, Edith. I've seen your house. Those doors and windows are old and brittle. There's no fence or boundary around the property. You don't have an alarm system." I shook my head. "And we don't have time to put all that in and bring it up to a minimum safe level. The Changs or Ana could make a move at any time."

"I don't care," Edith said. "Ana has robbed me enough already. I won't let her oust me from my home, too."

I glanced back. The little lawyer's mouth was set in a mulish line.

Josie shook her head but said nothing.

We pulled up to my shack, the headlights illuminating Tiki perched on the beach rock top step. The sensor light was on; the cat's movement must have activated it.

Tiki flattened her single ear and hissed, her kinked tail lashing. She glared at the van like it was a dragon boat filled with Vikings arrived to pillage.

I got out of the vehicle and shut the door carefully. "You're displeased with the lateness of my arrival, I see."

Behind me, I heard the murmur of voices. Hopefully, Josie would talk some sense into Edith.

I stepped up onto the porch and sidled warily past Tiki, who'd drawn blood for lesser infractions than being late. Making no sudden moves, I unlocked the door of the shack. Safely inside, I took a few minutes to refill Tiki's bowl with kibble and throw a change of clothes and my gun into an old gym bag for the overnight with Edith at Josie's house.

I left the Murphy bed strapped to the wall—no sense giving Tiki my pillow to sleep on—and made sure the lock was turned to secure the single window facing the jungle at the back of the shack. It wouldn't stop anyone determined to get in, though—that had already been proven.

The sad truth was, no lock or device was enough to keep out a determined intruder. As a Secret Service agent, I knew that better than most, and thus my recommendation that Edith be moved to a different location.

"Hopefully she and Josie have worked it out by now," I told Tiki, who was hunched over the bowl of food, crunching away. "Keep an eye on the place, will you?" I addressed her splotchy calico back, then eyed Miss Prissy the cane spider, who was perched in the corner nearest the bathroom. Tweedledum and Tweedledee, the geckos occupying their favorite spot above the stove, pumped their bodies up and down in comical push-ups, agreeing to my request. "I'll be back tomorrow after work. Thank goodness it's Friday. I'm ready for a weekend."

I locked Tiki and my "pets" inside. Tiki came and went freely through some unknown access point whose mystery I hadn't bothered to solve, and so did the others. They'd all be fine without me for a night. If it needed to be more, I could always call Opal and have her put food out on the porch for Tiki. The cat already had a water dispenser there.

Back at the van, I opened the front passenger door. "Did you ladies work it out? Seems like you needed a private moment," I said to Josie.

Josie shrugged, staring straight ahead, both hands on the wheel. She was not happy.

I hopped into the front seat, hauling my bag in behind me. "Okay, I guess you haven't worked it out yet. Edith?"

I glanced over my shoulder at the back seat. Edith was slumped over against the side of the van. Maybe she'd fallen asleep. Her hat was folded over her face. "Edith? Edith!"

She didn't answer.

I heaved myself into the rear of the van and ripped Edith's hat off, pressing my fingers to the older woman's neck to feel for a pulse.

9

EDITH HAD A PULSE—NOT strong but it was there, faint and thready. She was breathing. Maybe she'd just fainted.

"Josie, put this thing in gear and get us back to Hana to whatever passes as a hospital out here," I ordered. "Edith seems to have collapsed."

"Oh no!" Josie turned on the van with a rattle and then a roar. She turned up her oxygen flow, released the emergency brake, and put the van's shifter into reverse. "I thought she was giving me the silent treatment because I told her she should go along with your plan. I'm so sorry, Edie, honey!"

"I'm sure she'll be fine," I said soothingly, but I wasn't so sure as I sat on the bench seat and eased Edith over to rest her head on my lap. I fanned her pale face with the hat and patted her limp arms, calling her name and trying to wake her as Josie flicked on the van's lights and pulled out with a screech. She cranked the van onto Hana Highway and drove like an Indy 500 racer in a bad entry vehicle, taking hairpin turns on two wheels and downshifting the van's screaming old engine on the fly.

"You'll get her there faster than we would even be able to get a signal out to call for help," I yelled over the engine noise. "Great driving, Josie."

"I hope Edith doesn't need a real hospital," Josie shouted over her shoulder as she zoomed through a tunnel of trees on the narrow road. "Hana only has an urgent care. But they can airlift her to Maui Memorial if she needs more care than they can provide."

Fortunately, the little country road was empty of cars at this relatively late hour, and though I held my phone up frequently to try to get a few bars to call 911, nothing showed.

It was a short but harrowing trip, but we soon arrived at a single-story plantation style building in the heart of Hana. I was still unable to rouse Edith by the time Josie brought the van to a bumping halt outside the urgent care's lava front entrance.

"Come sit with Edith while I fetch help," I told Josie. She nodded and turned the van off, then squeezed between the front seats into the back. She took my place on the bench, tugging her oxygen tank into position as she seated herself. I got out of the way by cranking open the side door.

Josie lifted the other woman's head onto her lap. "Wake up, Edie," she said. "Please, wake up."

I left the van's side door open and ran up the wide steps into the building's double front doors. The place seemed deserted but for a lighted room down the main hall.

"Emergency medical assistance needed, stat!" I boomed. "I have an unconscious woman here!"

Several staffers in scrubs came hurrying out in answer. Soon, we had Edith moved onto a gurney and rolled inside the building. Nurses swarmed her, inserting an IV and placing an oxygen mask over her mouth and nose.

The doctor on call arrived to check her out and determined she needed to be sent to the emergency department at Maui Memorial. He called for a medical airlift, and before Josie and I had time to do much but watch with our mouths open, an ambulance arrived to take Edith to the airport. We hopped in the van and followed the ambulance to a helicopter landing area.

Soon a chopper arrived, landing on a nearby air pad. The helicopter took off for Maui Memorial Medical Center in Wailuku with Edith strapped into a transport bed inside the aircraft.

I turned to Josie. The elderly woman was wheezing and gray. I helped her over to a bench and summoned the EMTs to look her over, too. They recommended rest, oxygen, and no stress.

Josie snorted and began to cry. "What will I do without Edie?"

I patted her back, able to touch another human when I didn't know what else to do. "Is there anyone I can call for you?"

"Take me home and call Clara and Pearl to come over," Josie said. "I don't want to be alone."

"I agree with that a hundred percent," I said. I looped an arm around her and tugged her O_2 tank alongside us as I supported her back to the van.

Before I drove her home, though, I used the airport's landline to alert Sophie and Lei that Edith was being admitted to Maui Memorial and would need security there. Both were shocked but quick to respond—Sophie said she'd leave the Hotel Hana immediately and drive to Wailuku to watch over Edith tonight at the hospital. Her team would arrive in the morning to take over the lawyer's security. Lei was glad for the update, even though the news was bad.

I then called Clara from the Red Hat Society. She'd given her number to me when I asked about where she got her marvelous, draped clothing. Unfortunately, she designed and sewed it herself. (That ruled out getting anything to wear, of course. I'd sooner cook than sew, and that was saying something.)

"Clara, we've had an emergency. Can you and Pearl stay with Josie at her house? She's had a shock and isn't feeling well," I said. "Edith collapsed and has been taken to Maui Memorial Medical Center via airlift. I'm bringing Josie home now from the airport."

"Oh no. Of course!" Clara exclaimed. "We will see you there in a few minutes."

I took the wheel after making sure Josie was comfy resting on the bench seat in back with her oxygen flowing and a cool breeze hitting her face from the van's side window. As I drove, she issued directions to her house, which was up the hill past the church in Ohia.

I sighed with a deep sense of relief at seeing a familiar vehicle already there when we pulled into Josie's driveway. Clara's yellow Mazda Miata was hard to miss, even in the dark. The low, ranch-style house beyond it was hidden in a grove of hala and noni trees —both of which Josie taught me to identify.

"Now I know where to come on Tuesday nights for Hawaiian crafts," I told Josie as I parked the van in her lean-to garage. "I'm sorry I haven't made it over before this."

"You've had a few coconuts of your own to shuck," Josie said, hoisting herself upright. Her color was better, and when Clara opened the sliding side door, she mustered a smile for her friend. "Thanks for coming, Clara."

"Oh my dear. What a shock that must have been," Clara exclaimed, helping Josie and her tank out of the van. "Pearl couldn't come; her arthritis was acting up too bad. But she'll be here tomorrow."

I trailed after the women, instinctively checking the grounds for threats, but the isolated spot was peaceful and deserted. The moon shone high above while crickets chirped and bullfrogs brr-umphed from some hidden grotto.

That's when I remembered I was supposed to be going surfing with my favorite hot pilot on Saturday—and that wasn't going to happen. Instead, I needed to find a way to Wailuku tomorrow after work to check on Edith.

Keone Kaihale and I had been taking two steps forward, three stumbles back in a sort of dating situation. I was pretty sure I should give him a call about today's events. He'd told me that's what people in a relationship did. Not that we were in a "relationship," per se. But it was something, nonetheless, and he'd want to be informed.

I waited until Josie was settled in bed to ask to use her phone. "And I need some way to get home, too."

"Take the van," Josie said. "I won't be needing it for the next few days—I know when I need to stop and rest. You can take it to go check on Edith tomorrow after the post office closes. If you want to, of course."

"Thanks, Josie. That was exactly my plan. I really need to get myself a car. I'll go use the phone in your kitchen if you don't mind."

"Help yourself," Josie said. Clara was busy fluffing Josie's pillows, and the ladies barely acknowledged me as I gently closed the door.

I walked through the house to call Mr. K on the avocado-colored wall phone next to the fridge, feeling an uptick in my heart rate.

This was one phone call I was looking forward to.

10

ANA:

I lay in Fabio Chang's immense white bed, gazing out through the open sliders of his bedroom. The dude liked his white decor; maybe he knew how great it looked against his bronzed skin.

But now, moonlight filled the room, rendering everything in shades of gray, even the golden man beside me. A cold silver glow glittered on an ocean so far below it was like looking into black space—a little spooky.

I shivered.

Fabio's arm tightened around me. He flicked on the lamp beside the bed. "Chilly?"

"Just a little . . . surprised by how the day turned out." I turned on my side to face him, careful to arrange myself into a seductive and flattering pose. "I like the way you live."

"And I like the way you like the way I live." He kissed me, and it led to more, as it had from the minute he'd brought me upstairs to see the view.

You could say we connected, and you'd be right.

Later, I remembered I'd left Mom with the open bar in Fabio's living room. She was bound to be in a snit about it, even though

Fabio told me he'd sent a servant to tell her to take the car back down the mountain.

Fabio was sleeping. I rolled quietly out of bed and retrieved my phone from the charger on the side table—he'd thought of that too, the clever man. I was well on my way to liking him more than I should.

In the bathroom, I checked for messages. Sure enough, my inbox was cluttered with texts from Mom, ending with one that made me frown: *Since you've ditched me for your gangster boy toy, I'm going to Maui. I'll get our plan started myself.*

I didn't trust Mom to find her way out of a paper bag, let alone go to Maui and meet with her estranged mother, our hit target, Edith Pepperwhite.

I typed out a furious response with my thumbs: *Don't do anything, Mom. Go to that motel we were at and wait for me to get in touch with you.*

The text bounced back as *Not Delivered.*

I cursed. Mom must be somewhere out of cell service range— that meant a plane. Or maybe even Hana, though it was unlikely she'd had enough time to get there—but the phone service was notoriously spotty on the east side of Maui.

I went back to bed.

Fabio was awake. "You're worrying about your mother. It's cute."

I snorted. "Mom's a drunk elephant in a glass factory. I'm worried she'll mess things up. She texted that she's going to Maui."

Fabio held the covers open for me to slide in next to him. "Good. Your mom can draw the heat, while I send one of our best private contractors to take care of your Pepperwhite problem."

I embraced him. "Is it too soon to say, 'you complete me'?" I laughed to show I was joking.

He rolled me over. "No. I was wondering where you've been all my life, my lovely little psychopath."

When he said it that way, it sounded like a compliment.

11

KEONE KAIHALE LIVED in Hana in a small dark red-with-white trim cottage next to his mother's larger home. I'd been to Ilima Kaihale's home once before for an impromptu family luau, so I didn't need directions—but I was unsure if I'd found the right place, especially in the dark, until I spotted Mr. K's jacked-up green Toyota pickup parked in the lean-to garage.

Keone's truck type seemed to be the favorite transport for active men in Hawaii, but his was distinctive because of a miniature replica Hawaiian war helmet dangling from the rearview mirror that the van's lights picked up. I also recognized the surfboards we'd used on our last adventure strapped onto pipe racks built over the truck bed.

I parked the VW behind his vehicle and got out, carrying my duffel bag and the bottle of pineapple Maui wine Josie had foisted on me when she heard where I was going.

I wasn't entirely sure how I went from reaching Mr. K on the phone in Josie's kitchen to agreeing to go over to his place for a sleepover. Keone had expressed concern about my emotional and physical well-being as a reason for the visit, and it had persuaded me at the time.

Now I was feeling a distinct churning in the pit of my stomach that had nothing to do with the delicious dinner I'd consumed hours before at the Hotel Hana.

We'd spent the night together once before to no ill effect related to my touchphobia. The experience had been pleasant, but entirely platonic. I thought I could hear a little rasp in Keone's voice on the phone that told me he hoped it wasn't entirely platonic this time, and I hoped it wouldn't be either. But one thing I'd learned the hard way about my anxiety—pressure of any kind made it worse.

Keone must have been listening for the van's engine because he opened a screen door on the side of his house before I reached the doorstep. His short, curly black hair gleamed in the overhead light. "Come on in before the mosquitoes get you."

"It's definitely Maui midnight, as they call anything after eight p.m. around here," I said, slipping past him to enter. "I didn't see another car on the road."

"Yeah, things close early in Hana." Mr. K looked scrumptious, as usual. He wore a T-shirt and jeans, his typical non-work outfit. This particular shirt advertised a canoe paddling race five years ago, not that I noticed the way the faded logo stretched across his excellent chest.

"Thanks for having me over. I expected to be spending the night with Edith here in Hana, keeping an eye on her because of . . . well, what I've got to catch you up on. So I had a bag packed." I waggled my duffel. I didn't want to seem too eager.

He grinned. Good grief but he had a nice smile. It melted my insides like butter in the sun. "It seemed like you had a long, rough day and I thought this might be a good opportunity to practice more of that physical touch desensitization 'therapy' you told me about." He made air quotes with his fingers and winked. "I'm up for a challenge."

"Ah. Yeah. How about some wine?" I thrust the bottle at him awkwardly.

Mr. K held it up and grimaced. "MauiWine Pineapple? Seriously?"

"Josie insisted I bring something." My face felt hot. I looked around the room, anywhere but at him.

I'd seldom been in a man's house while we dated. Make that never, in fact. I didn't know what to expect. Keone's living room was nice, furnished with a rattan couch upholstered in denim and a couple of low, comfy-looking bentwood chairs angled to take in the big-screen TV on the wall behind a glass-topped coffee table. Mellow slack-key guitar filled the room from invisible speakers. I'd been learning about it from Artie Pahinui enough to recognize the unique island sound.

"You got any movies worth watching? I haven't seen anything since I got to Maui. The shack doesn't have a TV."

"Not until you catch me up on everything that's been going on. Did you have dinner?" Keone went into the small kitchen.

"Sophie and I had an early meal at the Hotel Hana before Edith and Josie got there and things went south." I patted my stomach.

"Let me pour you something better than this pineapple junk. Someone probably gave it to Auntie Josie, and she was happy to pass it on. Only tourists buy that stuff." Keone opened a cabinet above the fridge to reveal a range of bottles of beer, wine, and liquor. "Sometimes the guys come over for a game and we have a few."

"Nice setup for that," I agreed.

Keone grabbed a bottle of Pinot Noir and a corkscrew. He filled a stemless goblet for each of us. "I'll get us a snack, too."

"Perfect." I took my beverage and headed for one of the chairs. The denim slipcover was as soft as an old pair of jeans and seemed to embrace me as I sat. "Ah. This is nice." I put my size elevens on the coffee table. "I might not be able to stay up long enough for a movie, now."

"No nodding off until you tell me what's been happening."

Keone brought over a wooden plate piled with tortilla chips and a bowl filled with salsa and guacamole. "Let me know if you need anything more."

"Nope." I sipped my wine and reached for a chip, scooping some guacamole onto it. "Now what did I tell you so far?"

"Your friend Sophie appeared at the end of the workday with some news."

"Oh yeah."

I caught him up to the point of Edith's departure via chopper for the hospital in Wailuku. "Speaking of, can I use your Wi-Fi to call and see how she's doing?"

"Sure. But we all have landlines. The internet goes down a lot, even in Hana." Keone handed me a cordless handset. "Hopefully they have your name on the list of people who can find out about her condition."

"I hope so."

A few minutes later, seated on the couch with Keone's black phone in hand, I was connected with the nurse in the ICU. Thankfully, Edith had come around and given permission for the nurses to speak with Josie, Sophie, and me.

The news about Edith was not good. "Ms. Pepperwhite's had a heart attack," the nurse said. "She is in pre-op, preparing to have a procedure done to open the blockage in her artery. She is stable, and we expect her to tolerate the surgery well."

I took a moment to absorb this. "Are you aware that Ms. Pepperwhite has had threats issued against her life? Did our friend Sophie Smithson arrive to provide security?"

"Yes, and yes. We got a call from Maui Police Department to that effect, and we are cooperating with Ms. Smithson's presence here," the nurse said. "We're keeping Ms. Pepperwhite's name out of the computer system and using an alias for now, and your friend is watching outside the door."

"Good," I said, releasing a whoosh of breath. "Thank you so much for taking such good care of her."

After hanging up with the nurse, I immediately dialed Sophie on her cell. I couldn't wait to hear what my friend had to say about the current situation.

12

A MOMENT later I heard Sophie's husky British tones. "Kat, I'm glad you called. I just got here and positioned for security. I checked in with hospital security and the floor nurses to review their procedures, and it's all clear. Nothing threatening except Edith's own health, and she's stable for the moment."

"Well, that's something." I rolled my shoulders in relief. "She's where she needs to be then."

"Yes. Edith will be out of her procedure soon and settled in bed for the night. Everything seems quiet, and we've got her masked from the computer."

"Good. That's what the nurse was saying. I'm so glad you're on-site, Sophie. Unfortunately, I have to work tomorrow, but I'll drive out as soon as the post office closes at four p.m."

"The nurses are asking if you could swing by Edith's house and fetch her some personal items, maybe a sentimental photo or two, and a change of clothes and shoes for her to wear upon discharge," Sophie said. "Apparently it helps patients feel more positive to know their things are waiting for them."

"Sure. I'll go by her house after work and pack her a bag before

I drive out," I said. We sorted out a few more details and said goodbye.

I decided not to call and update Josie tonight. The elderly woman needed her rest, and besides, she could call the hospital herself if she wanted to.

I turned to Keone. He gazed back at me, warm brown eyes intent, a little crease of concern expressed by his brows. I was ready for whatever came next.

Or was I? My mouth was dry, and my heart was pounding, and it wasn't because I was worried about Edith.

I slid Mr. K's sleek black phone into its cradle on the side table. "You don't know how many avocado or beige landlines I've used since I moved to Ohia. Nice to see a newer phone for once."

"I enjoy the occasional modern touch," Keone said. "Want the grand tour?"

"Sure." I stood up, wine in hand, and followed Mr. K as he escorted me from the living room/kitchen to a short hall. "Office and guest room here."

I peeked in and was impressed with Keone's tidiness.

A daybed made up in a Hawaiian-print quilt occupied a spot under a large window. A sleek, modern desk and chair with a computer took up the other side, and a wall of bookshelves filled the middle. The floor was covered in woven hala matting, which I could identify thanks to Josie's culture lessons. The wall above the desk featured a poster of a determined looking Hawaiian man on a surfboard sliding down the face of a massive wave with the motto EDDIE WOULD GO at the bottom.

"Nice. Is that where I'll be sleeping?" I pointed to the daybed.

"I hope not." Keone gave me a long look full of promises. "Desensitization touch therapy, remember?"

I chickened out and broke eye contact. "Let's see the rest of your place."

"Not much to it," said my tour guide. He headed back into the hall. "Bathroom's between the bedrooms."

"I'll take a private minute here." I slipped inside, turning an old-fashioned lock on the door. Gripping the old-fashioned enamel sink, I stared at my reflection in the mirror above it. "Get a grip, Kat. You can pull the plug on this evening and go home anytime. Nothing's going to happen that you don't want to happen." Even so, I needed to pee, and then wash my hands, and then splash water on my face, and then take down my ponytail, and then fluff my long hair with Keone's comb for . . . reasons. I even brushed my teeth with my finger and a jot of toothpaste. Because maybe kissing. And germs. And freshness. And maybe kissing.

I opened the door. Keone stood outside, hands on his hips, that worried wrinkle between his brows. "You feeling okay?"

"Yep. Lead on, Macduff."

He shook his head. "I never understood that saying."

"Now it means 'you go on ahead and I'll follow.' But the saying was originally 'lay on, Macduff,' and it's from Shakespeare's Macbeth. It's an alteration of the famous phrase from the final fight scene where Macbeth lures his opponent into combat saying, 'Lay on, Macduff, And damn'd be him that first cries, 'Hold, enough!'" I made a dramatic gesture. "Aunt Fae put me in drama camp a few summers."

"So, you're equating me showing you my bedroom with being lured into a final fight to the death," Keone said.

"Um. No?" I scratched my head. "That's not what I meant—it's just a saying."

"Huh," he said.

I remembered I'd left my glass of wine on the sink. I darted back into the bathroom, grabbed it, threw back the wine like a medicinal shot, and returned to Keone's side. I burped behind my hand and held out the glass. "Refill, please."

"This isn't going well," Mr. K said as we went back into the living room. "Let's just watch a movie and you can go home."

Disappointment curdled my gut. Yeah, I was nervous about his bedroom. The fact that he had one. The room's mere existence prickled my skin. Also, more specifically, the likelihood of it containing a bed, which raised the hairs on my arms.

But heck yeah, I wanted to see it, at the very least. I was being a nincompoop, and that was unacceptable. I set the wineglass on the coffee table.

"Okay, then, I'll be Macduff and 'lay on.' Follow me, Mr. K, and upon your head be it." I spun on a heel, headed down the short hall, and flung open the bedroom door with a dramatic flourish.

Keone's bedroom was as inviting and uniquely Hawaiian as the rest of the house's decor. A pair of shiny wooden canoe paddles framed either side of the dark, carved-wood headboard of a king-size bed covered in a handmade quilt done in a red and white, stylized pineapple design. A closed closet door and a simple dresser in native koa wood completed the furnishings. A single pillow set right in the middle of the bed sent me a message as I gazed at it— no one shared this space with him.

Except, maybe me. If I chose to.

I could feel Keone arrive to stand beside me as if he had a magnetic force field around him, but we weren't touching at all. A wave of heat started at the top of my head and zoomed to my toes and back up again. I inexplicably wanted to hug him. Maybe more. A lot more.

But I felt weird too.

I fanned my face with a hand. "Keone. Oh my heck. Just looking at your bed, I'm feeling super anxious. My heart is pounding, I'm overheated, and my knees feel kinda wobbly. Maybe I should lie down. Do you have any ice water? A wet cloth for my forehead? Maybe I'm having a panic attack."

"And maybe—like the last time this happened—it's something else." Keone took my hand and gently turned me toward him. "Let's try a kiss and see. Would that be okay?"

"Sure. Okay." My heart sounded like thunder in my ears as I leaned in.

Well, let's just say whatever was going on with me wasn't a panic attack.

~

WE SPENT the night in that big awesome lovely comfy bed, and it wasn't platonic, though at least some of it was. I got enough sleep to wake up feeling ready to take on the world, and if I was still a virgin, enough had happened that I counted it a win.

"Hi," I said to his collarbone the next morning. "We're hugging. We've been hugging all night."

Keone chuckled. It was a rumble I felt through my whole mostly naked body. "A lot more than hugging."

"Yeah," I sighed. "I'm maybe—getting better from my touchphobia. At least with you."

"And what a therapeutic night it was." He tickled my ribs a bit, and I laughed and tickled him back. Soon we were wedged into the shower, which wasn't made for two, but we made it work.

He put on his awesome white uniform trimmed with blue stripes and gold braid. I put on my white polo shirt and stretchy black pants and brass postmaster name tag. We admired each other between sips of coffee as we stood in the kitchen. "You sure are good-looking," I told him. "That uniform. Yummy."

"Right back atcha, hot Postmaster Sleuth. When can we do this again? We need to make sure you're a hundred percent cured." He deployed his dimple. "We're on a roll here. So to speak."

"Ha!" I put down my mug, suddenly flustered. I remembered Edith in the hospital, and the Changs, and my job, and my cat who needed to be fed before work, and all the stuff that had disappeared from my brain for a lovely night of hugging (and more). "I'll call you. I gotta go." I grabbed my phone off his charger cord, picked up my Nikes and my bag, and ran out the door.

On the drive to Ohia in Josie's van, I thought about my boss's recent offer to post me to a special, all-woman security detail guarding the nation's first female Vice President. I'd turned it down, my "dream job," in favor of staying longer to solve the mystery going on with New Ohia, the Changs, and Edith's renegade grand-daughter Ana.

I'd been careful to inform Keone that I wasn't staying for him— but in the privacy of the van, with the sound of its noisy motor filling my ears as I navigated the narrow tropical route to Ohia, I admitted to myself aloud, "Keone's the cherry on the sundae of my reasons to be on Maui for a bit longer. I want to see how this whole thing goes."

I even hoped I might not be the world's oldest virgin for much longer.

But then what? That's when my imagination boggled.

My hands got clammy on the steering wheel as my gut twisted in a knot of old pain. I was barreling toward caring too much, and nothing lay in that direction but heartbreak. My parents' sudden death on an icy road taught me that the hard way.

I was better off alone.

I arrived at my shack, pulling up to park. There was no time to do anything about my depressing conclusion but run in, feed Tiki, and grab my keys to get the post office open on time.

13

THERE WERE days when I was grateful for my job as the only available employee at a post office that was the hub of a village. Today was one of them. I needed the busyness of a Friday as the solo operator of a two-person position to keep my mind off the repercussions of last night spent at Mr. K's house. Not to mention today's upcoming challenges, which would involve going to Edith's, packing her a bag, and heading out to Wailuku to check on her and her security. While I was at it, I should stay overnight on that side of the island because it would be dark by the time I got to the hospital.

If so, where would I stay?

All of those unfinished details were spinning around in my brain as I took a lunch break by putting a sign in the window— POSTMASTER ON BREAK, BACK AT 12:30—and headed over to the Ohia General Store.

The Pahinuis' store was cool, dim, cluttered, and as usual, smelled faintly of dust and dried beans (the source of that scent had never been evident—there were no open bins of beans). The premises were currently empty of customers.

Opal narrowed pale blue eyes at me from behind the big old cash register she no longer used, instead ringing up purchases on a tablet she was fingering. "Where were you last night? Because I heard from Clara who stayed out at Josie's about what happened to Edith. I know you weren't at either of their places."

I headed straight for the beverage cooler, opened the door, grabbed a bottle of root beer, twisted off the top, and took a long swig. I burped and took another swig, then wiped my mouth on the back of my hand. "Opal, I'm dying. I've had nothing to eat and only one cup of black coffee today to drink. What kind of sandwiches do you have? I'm on a half-hour break from the P.O., and I had to close the place to come get something to eat because I'm the only person on staff right now."

Opal's maternal instincts kicked in as I'd hoped they would, and her steely gaze melted in sympathy. "Oh, Kat, that's awful. You must be so stressed out. Artie made a big pot of chili today instead of sandwiches, and we've got fresh cornbread to go with it. Let me fix you a tray, and we can have a sit on the front porch. You can tell me all about what happened with Edith last night." Opal straightened today's capelike green velvet scarf over her shoulders, held in place with a giant shamrock pin. "And you can also tell me where you were last night." She bustled off, then tossed over her shoulder, "But I have a pretty solid guess where you were, since Josie's van, which you're driving, was spotted at Keone Kaihale's house."

"Can't slip anything past the coconut wireless." I was referring to the local gossip chain of which Opal was a primary link. I helped myself to a second root beer, having drained the first.

I needed to remember to take better care of myself. I was no use to anyone if I let myself get run down physically. And, I should probably be drinking water instead of my favorite sugary beverage, but I wanted an energy boost to get through the afternoon rush at the P.O.

Artie followed Opal out through the door marked Private that they used to access their attached home. "Need a little mood music while you eat, Kitty Kat? Also, I want the deets of your night, too."

I smiled at Artie as he made his way confidently through the store, holding his guitar cradled against his body as if it were a baby. It was easy to forget he was blind when he was in his own environment.

"Yes, music please." I followed him out through the store's front door. We sat on the worn wooden chairs on the porch. I turned my chair to avoid eye contact with the two or three customers lined up outside the locked post office door. "I hope Opal gets here soon with that chili and cornbread."

"Here you go, Princess Postmaster," Opal huffed. She plunked a bamboo tray onto my knees, loaded with a steaming bowl of chili sprinkled with cheddar cheese and a plate with two toasted, buttered squares of cornbread. A rolled set of utensils rested beside the food. "I'll put this and two root beers on your tab."

"About time Kat had a tab," Artie agreed, giving a dramatic strum on his guitar. "Now, what's going on with Edith? And where were you last night?"

Between bites, I told the couple what I knew about Edith and the security measures currently in place. "I haven't called the hospital yet to see how she's doing—I never had time this morning. Can I use your landline?"

Opal got up and went inside, then returned with a black cordless button phone and a third root beer. "I have the Maui Memorial Medical Center number right here." She rattled it off a fridge magnet she held as I punched the buttons.

I asked for the Intensive Care Unit and learned that Edith was still stable and resting comfortably. "We are monitoring her response to the procedure and will move her to a private room once we know she is out of the woods," the nurse in charge said. "Your female security operative has been replaced by a young man."

That must be one of Sophie's team members, so hopefully Sophie was getting a little rest. I hadn't forgotten how tired she'd already been when she had to hop in her car to drive out and guard Edith overnight.

"Thanks. I'll be in this evening to bring some personal things for Ms. Pepperwhite," I said. "What is her room number?"

"We're not giving that out at all. We will need to see your ID and escort you to her personally, and then you'll meet with her security guard," the nurse said. "So check in with the central nurses' station when you arrive, and we'll take you from there."

That process sounded reassuring for Edith's security. I thanked her and ended the call, handing the phone back to Opal. "Edith's stable and resting. I'll call again at the end of the workday and see how she's doing before I head out."

"Is she going to be safe there?" Opal stroked her shamrock pin as if to rub luck onto Edith.

"Yes," I said confidently, hoping I was right. "Edith wisely hired Security Solutions to keep her safe until the investigation into New Ohia is complete. Sophie was with her all night and her security team is there now. All the law enforcement agencies are looking for Ana. She's bound to turn up soon."

"Sounds like everything that can be done is being done," Artie said. "Now stop talking and start eating. You need your strength for the rest of the day." My friend bent over his guitar, plucking out a sweet song that relaxed my taut nerves.

I could take wise direction, kindly meant. I closed my eyes and listened to the beautiful island melodies he coaxed forth so easily for a long moment. I was so lucky to have Opal and Artie looking out for me.

I focused on finishing the rest of the chili and cornbread and accepted the third root beer from Opal. "Thanks so much. You two keep me going."

"It's mutual," Opal said, and patted my shoulder fondly. "We'll have to see what the runes have to say about all of this when we have time."

"Maybe right after I close up the post office? I don't want to miss out on that," I said. Opal had a gift for reading the shiny black kukui nut shells etched with ancient symbols that she carried around, and though sometimes the runes were maddeningly vague, I was fascinated with them and her process.

"If we can clear the store and get a private minute, I'm willing," Opal said. She jiggled the fabric pouch holding the shells where it resided in a hidden pocket of her dress. They made a soothing sound like a rainstick. "I'm setting my intention now."

"Good. I'll see you right after four," I told the Pahinuis, and hustled off the porch to deal with the gathering line of customers outside the main office doors.

As I unlocked the back door of the post office building, I grinned. In our concern over Edith, Opal and Artie had forgotten to bug me about where I'd spent the night. I didn't care if they knew, but I was glad I didn't have to talk about it—I wasn't ready to. Maybe I never would be.

What Keone and I had was too special to gossip about.

14

THE REST of my post office workday flew by. From the arrival of the morning's mail drop to all the sorting, waiting on customers, and giving out a large number of general delivery items, there was never a dull moment.

The Nakasone girls came in right at closing. Their long black hair hung unbrushed, tangled as yarn from a bad crochet project, and their clothes didn't look like they'd been washed all week. The older one, Sandy, stomped past the counter with nothing more than a stink eye.

Windy, maybe making up for her shorter stature, always gave more attitude, and today was no different. "I heard you're doing it with Keone Kaihale," she said without preamble, putting tiny fists on her hips. "He's out of your league."

I managed to cling to my Official Postmaster Face, which doubled as my Secret Service Professional Face. "That's none of your business," I said primly.

"I like Keone, and I'm going to marry him," Windy informed me. "Back off. He's mine."

I blinked. My mouth opened and closed but nothing came out. Finally I mustered, "How old are you?"

"Old enough to know what I want," she informed me.

Sandy passed by with the mail tucked under her arm and broke our stare down. She grabbed her sister's wrist, giving it a tug, with an eye roll to me. "Come on, Windy. You can get into that with her in ten years or so."

Two lollipops from a bag I'd found in Pua's desk and tucked into their mailbox were pressed tight against the envelopes, peeking out from under Sandy's arm. Treats were already earning me one ally, though it was unlikely that candy would soften Windy's jealous heart.

I waited until the two were out the door and halfway across the parking lot to scurry out from behind the counter and lock up. A quick moment to tidy up the place, and then I left the post office for the weekend. It was nice to have a job with such clear-cut boundaries for once.

I took a shower, changed, repacked my bag for another overnight, and fed Tiki. I gave the cat a scratch behind the ears as she grumbled into her kibble. "I know, girl. I'm going to be gone another night. You can always go over and visit Artie and Opal if you get lonely."

She twitched her tail irritably, expressing the inadequacy of their company, and I sighed. "I'll be back tomorrow after I take care of business with Edith in Wailuku. I promise."

The commitment of having a pet who wanted me around was new to deal with, and as I locked up the shack, I frowned. I wasn't certain I'd be able to get back tomorrow night if Edith needed me or something came up. But Tiki had been fine before I arrived—she'd be fine with me gone a few days.

I headed over to the general store. Opal had customers but gave me a head nod to indicate that I should man the front door and turn the sign to CLOSED. I did so, and she shooed the tourists lingering by the postcards and ice cream freezer out with a loud announcement that she was "Closing in five minutes!"

When the last of the sunburned visitors had been ushered

outside, I turned the lock on the door and returned to the checkout area. This time I grabbed a water bottle from the cooler. "Whew. Finally."

"Yeah. *Pau hana* at last." Opal already had her scarf spread out on the counter.

"Lei told me that means done working," I said.

"Yep." Opal shook the shiny black half shells out of their pouch into her palms, breathed on them, and without further ado, tossed them onto the velvet.

Three bounced off the counter immediately. "I don't even know how those got off the cloth," I said.

"They didn't want to be included." Opal picked up and put aside the three errant shells.

The store was so dim that I couldn't see the symbols etched onto the shells, so I turned on a green-shaded lamp near the cash register. Opal's short white hair caught the light like dandelion fluff as she bent, squinting over the shells, mere inches from their surfaces.

"Do you need your glasses, Opal?" I held out the magnifiers which rested on the base of the lamp.

"Oh, there they are!" Opal exclaimed and slid the glasses onto her nose. She hunched over again, perusing for a long moment. "Aha. I see traveling—someone traveling? And a female presence near the home symbol. Hmm. I hope that all means Edith will be coming home soon." She slid another of the runes, one that had fallen upside down, off to the side. "Let's see. Still danger and darkness in a prominent position. Perseverance and courage are needed. Multiple forces are working against each other, at cross purposes. But . . . the victory symbol is near the top of the reading." Opal looked up a me, blinking through the magnifying lenses. "Keep going with what you're doing, Kat, and it looks like things will work out in the end."

I was still pondering the reading, feeling both challenged and uplifted by it, when I turned the van into Edith's driveway and pulled up in front of her orchid-bedecked cottage. I frowned at the sight of an unfamiliar car. Edith's lime-colored electric vehicle was parked in the free-standing, open garage surrounded by flowering plants. A red Mustang, clearly a rental, was snugly tucked in behind it.

Could Ana have rented a vehicle and come here?

I reached into the duffel on the seat beside me and took out my weapon. I opened the VW's door and stepped out cautiously, keeping the vehicle's door between me and the porch of the house. "Hello? Anyone home?" I called.

A shadow moved behind the screen door, and it creaked open. A woman stood backlit in the doorframe, facing me. "Who are you and what do you want?"

15

THE SILHOUETTE STANDING in the doorway before me wasn't the medium height, shapely one that belonged to Ana Davies, but it did have a familiar look. "I'm Kat. A friend of Edith's. I'm here to get some things for her stay at the hospital. And you are?"

"Mother's in the hospital?" The woman came forward out of the shadows. She was blonde, about four foot, eleven inches in height, and had the same barrel body and bright blue eyes as Edith. "I'm Edith's daughter. My name is Lola Reeves." In all the hullabaloo about Ana and the discussions about Edith's child, I'd never heard her daughter's name.

My threat assessment put Lola Reeves at Level 2.5 out of a possible 10. This woman wasn't going to make a move and if she did, I could flip her down the stairs faster than a gecko could do a push-up.

But Ana could be lurking inside the house, and she was more of a concern. Lola had to know what her daughter was up to and might be in on it. Until I knew more, best to make nice.

I slid the gun out of sight into a handy pocket. I advanced with a big fake smile and an extended hand. "Kat Smith, Postmaster. What brings you out here to Hana?"

Lola's handshake was damp and doughy, and her nails were long, bright, and elaborately bejeweled. No manual labor for this lady. "I came to visit my mother. I was so upset by what Ana was up to. I wanted to let Mother know I had nothing to do with it."

I glanced past Lola to the ripped screen and shattered pane above the handle of the front door. "So you broke into her house?"

Lola shrugged. Her eyes had a glassiness about them that was concerning. Drugs? "She wasn't home."

I was standing close enough to catch a whiff of alcohol on her breath. Not drugs. Edith's liquor cabinet.

"Well, in a way you're here at the perfect time," I said. "Edith's had a little heart episode. I'm here to pick up some things for her." I pushed past Lola and opened the door, scanning for any sight of Ana.

Nothing out of place in the comfortable living room except the cabinet where Edith kept her liquor bottles—that door was ajar. Through the entry to Edith's bedroom, I spied a large suitcase on the bed.

"How bad is it?" Lola's tone changed from flat to highly interested. "Is she going to die?"

I wheeled on my size elevens and narrowed a stare at her. "You sound pretty eager for that to happen."

Lola blinked but didn't back down. "I'm her heir, you know. It's natural that I'd be . . . concerned."

"I can see that," I said drily. I remembered Edith telling me she'd made her will out to her daughter as a gesture of reconciliation. Hopefully, she wouldn't regret that decision. "Well, I'm going to pack Edith a bag. I could bring you with me. I'm sure it would mean a lot to Edith to see you." If Lola agreed, I could keep a close eye on her. Maybe she'd lead us to Ana.

"I'll stay right here and wait for her," Lola said, and plopped into Edith's recliner facing the big-screen TV. "She'll have something to look forward to when you tell her I'm here." She reached for a cut crystal glass of liquor on the side table and took a sip.

I ground my back teeth together but kept my opinions to myself. I headed for Edith's room, still vigilant for signs of Ana. Was there anything I could I do about Lola squatting in her mother's house?

Lola wasn't on the lam from police. As far as I knew, she didn't have a criminal record, though we would certainly check. She was definitely who she said she was. One look at her was enough to confirm her identity as Edith's daughter. And though I felt confident Edith wouldn't want Lola camping out in the house, drinking her booze and eating her food, even if I called the police, I doubted there was anything that they would do about an unclear family dispute.

I scanned the suitcase on the bed. It was a Louis Vuitton knockoff with peeling corners. The closet was already open, and Edith's shoes and clothing had been jostled about. Lola was probably looking for money or jewelry.

My neck was tight with anger as I found a set of petite flannel pajamas and some fuzzy slippers and put them on the bed for Edith. I went to the dresser and took out underthings and a bright purple track suit that would go with my friend's red hat. "I'll let Edith know you're here the minute I speak to her," I said over my shoulder. "You should have her permission to stay here."

Lola snorted from her throne in the living room. "Mother owes me, and she knows it."

What would happen if I grabbed this awful little woman by the scruff of the neck, threw her into that rental Mustang by force, and made her leave at gunpoint? I was certainly strong enough to do that. But Lola would probably lodge a "threat with a deadly weapon" charge and come right back to the house the minute I was gone. I knew her type: quick to sue or file a complaint, always a victim, and sticky as gum on a shoe to deal with.

I found an old-fashioned carpetbag at the back of the closet and stuffed the clothing and a pair of sensible pull-on walking flats inside. On impulse, I grabbed a spiral notebook and pen I spotted on the side table. If Edith kept a diary, I didn't want her daughter reading it.

Done packing, I went to the phone on the dresser, thumbed through my cell for the number, and called Josie's house.

Josie answered immediately. "Edith? Is that you? Are you home?"

I hated to crush the hope in her voice as she must have seen the familiar number on her readout. "No, Josie, it's Kat. I'm here packing up some things for Edith at the hospital and her daughter Lola is here and planning to stay."

"Who are you calling?" Lola shrieked from the living room. "Put that phone down immediately! You don't have permission to use our appliances!"

"Oh no! Edie and I talked about changing her will, but she hadn't got around to it yet. Has Lola taken anything?" Josie wheezed in distress.

"Not sure," I said in a bright neutral tone. "I thought you and the other Red Hat ladies should know. Maybe you can come check on the house. Water the plants and feed Butter."

"I see where you're going with this," Josie said.

"I'm in charge here. No other help is needed." Lola arrived in the doorway, red-faced. She shook a wine key at me with the curly, pointy end extended threateningly. "Hang up that phone and get out of our house!"

I ignored her. "Meanwhile I'm getting on the road to Wailuku," I went on. "I'm sure you heard Edith is recovering well from her procedure and should be home in a day or two."

"I heard no such thing," Josie protested. "They said she's not out of the woods yet. I have my prayer group doing shifts that she makes it through the night!"

"Edith will be so excited to see everyone as soon as she gets back," I forged on. "All her friends at the police department will be swinging by to check on her place in the meantime, too, right?"

"Riiiiiight." Josie finally got the drift. "Good idea. I'll call my friend at the Hana PD and see if he can go by and rattle Lola's cage."

"Okay, sounds great. I'll get going now. Bye." I hung up. I picked up the carpetbag and stalked toward Lola, fire in my eyes.

She backed up and stumbled as she did so, scrambling around to get the recliner between us and brandishing the wine key like a sword. "I don't like you!" she hollered.

"The feeling's mutual. If you take anything from this house, you will be prosecuted to the full extent of the law," I said. "Edith will be back soon. She won't be happy you've been sleeping in her bed and drinking her booze, but I'll give you the benefit of the doubt for the moment. Now. Where's Ana?"

"What?" Lola fell into the recliner and clutched her empty glass to her chest. "Ana? I have no idea. We had a f-f-falling-out." She burped. "That girl can't keep her pants zipped. She'll have to learn the hard way, like I did."

Staring down at Lola, I had an intuition that it was this woman who would be taught a lesson by her much more ruthless and scarier daughter. "You'd better be gone by the time Edith gets home," I growled, and stomped out.

My shoes made a hollow sound on the floor that was as empty as my threat.

16

ANA:

After a leisurely beginning, Fabio and I spent the day reviewing his plans for New Ohia.

"I'll take you to my office and show you what we're planning, if we could just get the FBI off our backs," he said as we drove down the mountain in his bulletproof black SUV. The floor of his subsidiary of Chang Enterprises was located in a sleek modern building that gave nothing away from the outside—not so much as a street number marred the tall building's liquid-metal silhouette.

I was glad he'd had some clothing delivered for me—the personnel and environment was as sophisticated and upscale as anywhere on the continent. "Come see the scale model of New Ohia." He led me into a big boardroom whose table was taken up by an architect's 3D rendering. "That's my house. On the top of the hill."

I straightened the sleek sheath dress he'd bought me with its matching pair of lace-up heels. Striking a pose, I leaned over to inspect a miniature Greek-style mansion with its own pool. "Very nice." I caught him checking out my behind, as I'd intended. "You have good taste."

"Of course I do." He winked. We understood each other. "Maybe you'll buy into New Ohia when you come into your inheritance," he said, spinning a bullet-shaped metal pen on his palm. "Hopefully that's sooner rather than later."

"Or maybe I'll hang out at your pool when we both feel like it," I said. "After all, can't count chickens that haven't hatched. Speaking of, what's your plan to get rid of the FBI investigation?"

"Eliminate our paper trail, which I've already done for the most part. Get rid of opposition and witnesses. The FBI probe won't find anything but a black hole."

I hopped up onto a black onyx desk and swung my sandaled legs. I could see several issues with this blunt-instrument approach. "But I heard a group of investors got wind of the scam and were behind a new complaint."

He walked away restlessly. "I refunded those people's money and paid them extra to walk away. I also made sure they knew who they were dealing with if they talked to the Feds. The complaint has been removed and they've recanted."

"Then you can move forward if the community resistance goes away," I said in wonderment.

"Why do you think it's so important that Edith Pepperwhite is shut down? Without her, the community noise will die down. It's like so many shady developments in Hawaii. Once the people accept it happening, we 'pave paradise and put up a parking lot.'" He smiled.

"That old Joni Mitchell song." I crooked my finger at him. "Until you explained this to me, I thought you'd be lucky to keep the money you stashed in those offshore accounts. Now it's looking like you'll be able to build that pretty house on the hill, too."

"There are still a few flies in the ointment." Fabio answered my summons by coming to stand between my knees. My skirt was too tight to allow much movement, but he didn't seem bothered by that as his hands wandered. "I'm glad I have you as a partner in getting rid of them."

I was glad, too, and decided to show it without words.

17

"SON OF A COTTONTAIL." I squeezed the worn plastic steering wheel of the van repeatedly, releasing frustration as I drove toward Wailuku. Even so, it took me over an hour of the drive to calm down after my encounter with Lola at Edith's cottage.

I was glad of how challenging the infamous "road to Hana" on Maui was because the pretty, tropical obstacle course forced me to concentrate. As close to dark as it was, the narrow passage was busy with tourists returning to civilization and locals pressured for time.

Driving Josie's rattletrap VW van, I considered myself in the latter group as I navigated a route that was both a sightseeing event and a vital transportation artery for those who lived on the remote east side of the island. It took all my defensive driving skills and a lot of shifting to stay in my lane (especially when there was only one) so I couldn't mentally grind too much on the frustrating events that had taken place at Edith's house.

I'd bet my precious Nikes that Edith would not want her daughter camping in her place, and I'd left Lola sipping a drink in her lounger. In hindsight, I'd also missed an opportunity to thoroughly search the house and grounds for Ana. Lola's daughter could have been in one of the closets chuckling at me and her mother for all I knew. I could kick myself for letting my emotions get in the way of a thorough search. Hopefully, whoever Josie knew at the Hana Police Department would be able to go by and "rattle Lola's cage" as she'd put it.

But most of all, I was worried for Edith. I hadn't missed Josie's comment that my lawyer friend was not out of the woods yet.

Full dark had fallen and over two hours passed by the time I pulled up and parked Josie's van at Maui Memorial Medical Center in Wailuku. I went to the front desk as the nurse had directed me to do, and after checking my ID and a list of admitted visitors, a staffer led me upstairs to the fourth floor. She turned me over to a nurse at the main station there, and after another check, the nurse took me to a room at the end of the hall.

I was relieved to see an operative clad in a set of scrubs (in order to blend with the staff) sitting outside the door. The dude checked my ID a third time and matched my name to a list on his phone, and finally I was admitted to the inner sanctum. I gently eased the door open to the dimly lit room.

Edith was sleeping. She looked frail in the hospital bed in the center of a web of beeping machines and fluid and medication lines. I took a plastic chair and sat beside her, checking her over as I did so. Her color was bad, and she was on oxygen but breathing on her own. The room wasn't in the ICU, so she must be stable.

A hand rested on the sheets beside her body, palm up. An IV occupied her opposite hand, so I took the one closest to me. It felt limp, cold, and bony. I resisted the urge to drop it back onto the bed. I could touch her. I would touch her. Touching an ill person was good. I could do this.

Edith was a small woman, but she looked tiny now, shrunken from her sturdy dimensions by the physical challenges of the last few days. After a suitable interval, I released her hand. That must've been enough to wake her, because Edith's blue eyes, as bright as her daughter Lola's, fluttered open. She tried to speak but winced—it looked like her throat was sore.

"Do you want some water?"

She nodded.

I picked up a plastic container with ounces marked on the side and a straw in it. I held the straw to her lips, and she drank. I set it back down and patted her hand where it lay on the sheets. "Don't talk, just rest." She captured my hand in hers, and this time, the life in her fingers gave me the strength to squeeze back. "I wanted to come see you. How are you doing?"

Edith nodded and blinked; her mouth trembled. Her white hair was a disorderly cloud of fluff on the pillows.

"I take it that means you're about as good as can be expected after a heart attack and an operation, right?" I rubbed the back of her hand gently with my thumb; the skin was thin and papery. "I have some news. Your daughter Lola turned up at the house, and she refused to leave. Are you okay with her staying there?"

Edith's eyes widened. She opened and closed her mouth again. I reached for the cup of water with the straw and held it for her again. She drank thirstily and cleared her throat. This time, she was able to speak. "Who?"

"Lola. Your daughter. She was already at your place when I went by to your house to get a few things for you." I indicated the b ag I had brought. "She had broken in."

"Was Ana there?" Edith croaked.

"I was too distracted to search thoroughly, but I didn't see any signs of her. Lola claimed they had a falling-out."

Edith nodded and made a spinning gesture with her hand for me to go on.

I rubbed my nose, uncomfortable. "Lola had been drinking. She refused to leave when I suggested she come with me to visit you. She said Ana wasn't with her and she didn't know where her daughter was. I called Josie and asked her to swing by and check on the house and ask her friend at the Hana PD to go by, too. But I'm pretty sure the police won't do anything about her being there unless you call and ask them for help."

Edith closed her eyes. The effort to focus seemed to have exhausted her. I picked up the water and brought the straw to her lips again, and she drank more. This time, her voice was a little stronger when she spoke. "It's okay if Lola is there, as long as Ana isn't."

"I think she went through your closets," I said. "She was definitely making free with your liquor cabinet. Are you sure?"

"I owe her," Edith said.

That was exactly what Lola had told me. There was much between mother and daughter that I knew nothing about, and it was none of my business.

Talking was exhausting her, so I patted her hand again. "I will let Josie know that Lola has your permission to stay there. Don't worry about it."

Edith seemed to slip away. Her mouth fell open. Soft regular breathing filled the room.

I had an answer, even if it wasn't the one I'd expected. I left, pausing to speak with the operative. "Where is Sophie staying?"

"She might be at our headquarters, an office in the Cameron C enter nearby," he said. "Or, Ms. Smithson is with a police officer friend of hers." That had to be Lei, and now I knew exactly where to go to spend the night tonight.

As I'd hoped, Sophie picked up right away when I called on speakerphone while driving away from the hospital. Lei chimed in. "Come on over and eat! You're welcome to bunk in the spare room with Sophie."

Man, it felt good to have friends. My heart lifted as I turned the van toward the lush area of Haiku, where Lei and her family lived.

18

"Breakfast's ready, aunties." Kiet, Lei and Stevens's young son, had a piping voice that woke me immediately. I lifted my head from where I'd sunk deep into an inflatable mattress and slept like a hibernating bear. "Thanks. We'll be right there," I called.

Sophie slumbered beside me, in the twin bed of Lei's small guest room/office. She hadn't moved, so I reached up from my spot on the floor and poked her. "Rise and shine, Madame CEO."

She groaned. "No, thank you."

I felt her pain.

Lei, Sophie, and I had been up late last night, polishing off a bottle of red wine at the picnic table under the mango tree, and catching up on our personal lives with no mention of the case allowed. It was one of the first times I'd been a part of a no-holds-barred, women's "henfest," as her husband Stevens called it.

"Thank goodness it's Saturday." I wallowed out of the squishy mattress and hoisted myself upright, pulling on a pair of yoga pants and a tee.

"Security Solutions pays no mind to days of the week," Sophie muttered, sitting up. She cradled her head. "I seldom drink. This headache is unpleasant." Her short, cropped hair was hardly mussed, and she was too beautiful to need makeup, but there were tired shadows around her eyes. "I shouldn't have indulged."

"You're the CEO of your company, and Edith is being protected by your minions. Sleeping in is allowed, and so is drinking. Also, I smell coffee. And pancakes." I padded off in search of food. Lei had fed me leftovers when I arrived late last night, but I burned calories like a coyote on the hunt. I was ready for more.

Lei and Stevens had set the picnic table outside for breakfast. Even though a big mango tree shaded it, the sun was already warming up the dewy grass. I slid my feet into a spare pair of rubber slippers and padded with their Rottweiler Conan around to the back of the house, where I could see the great purple-gold hump of Haleakala with the sun breaking over its shoulder.

Lei's grandfather Soga lived nearby in a cute, tiny house. The old man, mid-eighties if he was a day, was already outside with a fruit picker, pulling down bumpy red fruits from a tree near his miniature abode. I'd met these walnut-size delicacies called lychee before on one of my foreign missions, and they were a favorite.

I hurried over, reaching for the picker he held—a long bamboo pole with a cut bleach bottle tied to one end. "Let me help."

Soga looked me over from behind thick glasses. "Your arms are skinny."

I laughed. "But I'm tall. I can reach higher than you."

"Yes you are."

"Then, let me try, sir. Please."

"Because you asked nicely." He surrendered the picker, and I was able to bring down a few high clusters with his help when I heard Stevens call, "Food's on the table!"

"We should get some before it's gone." Soga scooped the fruit out of the picker into a pail. "This family eats fast. Always in a hurry, you know."

"I hope not today," I said. "It's Saturday. *Pau hana*, they say. No work."

He shook his head. "Murder never sleeps."

Sobered by that reminder, I followed the octogenarian back to the outdoor table, carrying the pail of lychees.

A giant stack of pancakes on a platter decorated the middle of the table, along with a wood calabash of tropical fruit salad and a bowl of scrambled eggs. I grabbed a disposable plate and piled it high, taking a seat on the bench beside Lei's tall, blue-eyed spouse.

"Thanks for the hospitality," I said. "This looks delicious."

"Saturday morning tradition. An antidote to the busy week for our whole family." Stevens handed me a pot of honey with a spoon in it. "This local avocado honey is great with the fruit or dribbled on the pancakes."

I needed no further instruction.

Over breakfast, I met a few more people: Lei's father Wayne Texeira, a handsome older man with a look of Carlos Santana about him and his partner—a slender blonde woman named Ellen, who happened to be Stevens's mother.

"Well, that worked out nicely," I commented. The couple's happiness was obvious as they laughed.

Lei handed me the coffee carafe. "We thought so too. Nothing better for the kids than having their grandparents nearby and my grandfather, too."

Soga nodded sagely from his perch in an armchair at the head of the table.

"You're so lucky," I said. "I only have my Aunt Fae, and she's six thousand miles away."

"I share your feeling." Sophie said. "I don't have extended family around me either, but I have friends who are like family. And now you have us, too."

"Thanks." I stared at my pancakes, blinking like mad because dust got in my eye.

After the meal was eaten and the table was cleared, the family dispersed to their various Saturday activities. Lei, Sophie, and I returned to the picnic table with fresh mugs of coffee.

"So, what's today's plan?" I asked.

"Why don't you fill us in on the latest that's going on with Edith?" Sophie asked. "You said there was a surprise out at her house."

"There have been some new developments," I said. "Edith has a squatter in her house. Ana's mother Lola turned up and made herself at home. Strangely, Edith gave permission for her to be there." I filled the two women in on what happened the previous day. "The worst is that I missed an opportunity to thoroughly search the premises for Ana."

"It's not too late for that to happen," Lei said. "Let me make a call."

She pulled out her phone and was soon in touch with a friend at the Hana PD. An officer was dispatched to check the premises for the fugitive Ana Davies. They'd call back and report who was there.

Lei ended the call and looked at me. "Why didn't you do that yesterday?"

It hadn't crossed my mind and I wasn't sure why. Heat burned my cheeks. "All I can say is that I'm used to handling situations myself. I got distracted."

"You've got a team now. Use it," Lei said.

Sophie bumped me with her shoulder. "Speaking of using items—you seem to need a reliable vehicle. I'm going back to Honolulu later today and usually park my Security Solutions SUV in a storage lot. Want to drive it until you get something of your own?"

"Can I hug you?" I exclaimed.

"Of course," Sophie said, and I did.

"Now let's get down to business," Lei said. "We need Marcella on the phone to update us on what's going on with the FBI investigation into New Ohia. Let's video call her if I can get enough bars out here." Lei propped her phone up against a salt shaker and hit dial for Special Agent Marcella Scott, who was heading up the investigation into the backdoor deals that led to New Ohia.

As the phone pulsed its signal, a toddler with a full head of brown curls trundled down the front steps and ran toward us.

"Auntie Kat!" Rosie, a cherubic toddler whom I had driven home one memorable day, popped her thumb out of her mouth to greet me before embracing her mother's knees and scrambling up onto Lei's lap.

"Special Agent Scott." Marcella's voice was all business until she got an eyeful of Rosie and Lei in her video screen. "Well, hello, sweetie! And Lei too, of course."

"Auntie 'Cella," Rosie said.

Marcella laughed. "Yes. And who else is there?"

"Auntie Kat and Auntie Sophie," Rosie said.

"And now it's time for grown-up talk," Lei said, sliding the little girl to the grass and patting her diaper-padded bottom. "Go bug your papa while we talk police business."

"No. Rosie stay with Mama." Eventually, the two-year-old had to be hauled off by her aforementioned papa, wailing and thrashing.

"Yikes. I'm definitely not ready for kids," I said, watching them go.

"There are a lot of days like that," Sophie agreed. "That's why I love having a nanny when I'm working."

"Wish we had one too, but Wayne and Ellen help out a lot," Lei said. She took out a small spiral notebook and pen. "Let's not waste valuable time. Marcella, bring us up to speed on the investigation at your end, and then we'll fill you in on developments over here."

19

After the meeting, I drove Josie's van toward the Maui Memorial Medical Center parking lot as Sophie followed me in the white Ford Explorer I'd be using.

Every time I glanced in the rearview mirror and glimpsed the SUV's unassuming profile with Sophie at the wheel, I felt a wave of gratitude. Not just for her generous offer to use the car, but for the friendship of the three amazing women I was getting to know through the investigation.

At Lei's picnic table, Marcella had filled us in on the FBI's progress. "We have documents showing that the lease the state made to the corporation does not enable them to sell the lots in the development. The title company working with them is likely a front because it's been generating false documents that make buyers believe they now own their lots and houses outright, when what's really going on is that New Ohia Vision owns them."

"I thought that's what I'd read on the documents I obtained," I said. I'd broken into one of the model homes in the New Ohia subdivision and found a memory drive left behind by the development's deceased coordinator. That had been a breakthrough in understanding what was going on. "How close are you to shutting the development down?"

"Unfortunately, New Ohia Vision's been siphoning the cash through offshore corporations and hiding it overseas," Marcella said, her face a dark silhouette in a backlit view on her computer on Oahu. "The FBI has frozen their U.S. assets, though, so their current operation can't keep going much longer. They'll run out of money."

"That ought to put an end to that poser Thompkins throwing his weight around at the development," Lei said. "Kat ran into some difficulty with the security team there."

I flapped a hand. "All's well that ends well, but I'll be glad when Thompkins is gone. He's been doing his best to pretend everything's normal, even ordering a big postcard campaign to generate new sales."

"Well, his funds will be drying up soon," Marcella said. "We're focusing on getting control of that money and following it to the real players."

"Do you think Edith is still in danger?" I asked.

"Yes," Lei, Sophie, and Marcella all said at once.

I smiled involuntarily at the sound of their chorus, though the situation wasn't funny.

"We've heard chatter online confirming there's a hit out on Edith. The Changs are rumored to be behind it, but as I said earlier, Ana Davies is aligned with them," Sophie said. "Even though the FBI's making some progress, Edith remains the figurehead of legal opposition. Without her and her research and testimony, the case could fall apart."

"What role do you think Edith's daughter, Lola Reeves, plays in all this?" I asked. "She's camped out at Edith's house, claiming she and Ana parted ways and are not working together."

"The Hana PD will be doing a thorough search of Edith's place," Lei said.

"When I was there, I saw no evidence Ana was ever on the

property," I said. "Lola told me that she was waiting for her mother and looking after her home in the meantime. But I seriously doubt the woman's capable of taking care of anything but her own thirst for booze."

"I've run a deep background on her," Sophie said, her fingers flying on a small laptop. "Nothing on Lola but the bad credit of a woman who's been through three divorces and never figured out a personal direction."

"We should keep close tabs on Lola, regardless," Lei said. "I'm not convinced there's been a falling-out between her and Ana. They could be communicating."

"I agree," I said. "I think Lola is hoping Edith will die so she inherits her estate. We have to get Edith to change her will. I will work on that angle with her."

"Lei, Sophie, and Kat, why don't you focus on finding Ana Davies and keeping an eye on Lola?" Marcella asked. Her voice fizzed a bit in the connection. "We have a lot to do here behind the scenes, going after the bigger fish and getting the New Ohia Vision corporation shut down. Too much to do to chase Ana, who's not a player in the main investigation."

"Okay, we'll focus on Ana here on Maui," Lei agreed, and we wrapped up the call.

My reverie had been so engrossing that, driving on autopilot, I'd already turned past the big urban building that housed the Maui Police Department and was heading to the smaller Cameron Center below the hospital, where the Security Solutions firm had an extension office.

I parked Josie's van in front of the security firm's low-profile digs, located a few hundred yards from the hospital. I got out, locked the van, and hid the keys on a back tire. I'd already called Josie to update her on events and let her know where her vehicle was going to be for pickup. She was planning to come out and visit Edith today, driven by Clara, and would be picking up the van.

"And please, try to get Edith to take Lola off her will," I implored. "I have a bad feeling about their motives."

"Definitely," Josie agreed. "I'll try to get her to do that. But she's stubborn, you know."

"Oh, I know." That stubbornness might get Edith killed, but I'd do my best to keep that from happening.

Sophie pulled up beside me in the white SUV and got out, carrying a leather messenger bag that looked like it held the secrets of the universe. "I have to run into the office and check with the staff about our cases. Want to come in and see our operation?"

"Yes, please," I said, and bounded after my long-legged friend as she took the outside stairs two at a time.

The Security Solutions workspace was light, bright, and minimalist, consisting of a single open work area with four desks separated by shoji blinds, with a conference table in the center. The workroom was entered through an exterior waiting area with an unattended reception desk.

Sophie gestured to the monitor in the center of the conference table. "Security Solutions ended up needing an office here on Maui, but we end up mostly using video for meetings." She gestured to the young man I'd met in the hospital, seated at one of the desks. "This is Chance Wakea, one of our operatives."

"We've met, though we didn't exchange names." I shook the man's hand briefly. "How's Edith doing today? I'm going up to visit her after I take Sophie to the airport."

Wakea's brows drew together in a frown. "She's not doing so great today. She's running a fever. And that was before we had an attempted breach of the room, which stressed her out."

"What!" Sophie and I exclaimed. Sophie took out her phone, scowling at a series of missed calls. "Looks like you tried to reach me."

"Of course." Wakea pushed a hand through military-short black hair. "We were lucky. The attempt happened as Trey—that's our other staffer—came to relieve me. The suspect was disguised as a hospital staff member in scrubs and a mask. He came up to us with some equipment, claiming to need to do a minor procedure on Edith. We'd been given copies of the ID badges of all of the hospital staff, and I realized there was something off when the staffer refused to pull down his mask for our ID check. He then ditched the equipment and ran off. I stayed with Edith, while Trey tried to run him down. The perp made it to the stairs and got off at a different floor and was able to lose Trey."

Sophie and I exchanged worried glances. "That attempt might have worked if both of you hadn't been there and they'd sent in a second person," I said. "Do you think two operatives is enough, Sophie?"

"No," Sophie said. "And now we need to move Edith to another location if that's possible with her health condition. Let me make some calls. I know you've been up all night with our client, Chance, but could you go stay at her room with Trey until I pull in some more staff? We have to take this threat seriously."

"Yes, especially because the suspect left behind a loaded syringe. We sent it to the hospital's lab for analysis, right after we called the police to report the incident," Chance said. "They haven't gotten back to us with analysis yet, but we suspect something deadly was in it."

"What did the police say?" I asked, curious.

"The 911 dispatcher told me they'd alert Sergeant Lei Texeira, the detective on the case," Chance said. "They thanked me, too. Said they were glad Trey and I were there, even if we didn't get the guy."

"Yes. Good job keeping Edith safe," I said. "That's the priority, right, Sophie?"

Sophie nodded, her fingers flying on a tablet she held as she spoke rapidly into a phone earpiece. "Reinforcements are on their way, Chase."

"And I'll come up too, as soon as I take Sophie to the airport," I said. "She's going back to Oahu."

"Aye, ma'am." The young man tossed a salute in our direction as he headed for the door at a jog.

Sophie rolled her eyes. "Ugh. I've officially crossed the 'ma'am' threshold," she said. "I'm getting old."

"That must have been meant for me," I said. "People always think I'm older."

Sophie smiled. "And how old do you think I am?"

"No idea. You could be anywhere from twenty to fifty," I said truthfully.

"Good. Then I'll let that remain a mystery. And in the meantime, would you like a job?"

"I already have a job. Secret Service agent temporarily assigned as postmaster."

"But when you're not at that job, would you like to work for me? Or I should say, for Security Solutions? As an independent contractor on call." Sophie tossed me the keys to the SUV. "You're already driving the company car."

20

I took Sophie up on her offer of additional employment; I knew a good thing when I saw it. If Sophie wanted to throw money at me for what I'd have done for free, who was I to decline?

She pulled up a contract for me to sign as an independent contractor, and we spent the drive to the airport strategizing my new role. "I want you to be on call as a consultant for our celebrity and sensitive protection cases on Maui when you're off duty from the post office," she said. "It's not every day I get the expertise of a top Secret Service agent to call upon."

That was gilding the lily a bit, but I didn't argue. I dropped her off for her flight to Oahu. As she walked away, I peeled the magnetic signage identifying the vehicle as belonging to Security Solutions off the doors and threw the rolled-up logo in the back. Advertising our presence wasn't smart in this situation.

At the hospital, I directed Trey, Chance, and the hospital staff in an additional layer of security protocols that should help avert another attempt on Edith's life while she lay vulnerable in a public institution. The hospital administration required some wrangling, but the threat of a lawsuit was enough to get them to comply. These things included Security Solutions operatives remaining disguised in hospital scrubs, and relocation of Edith to a more secure floor. As we trundled my friend's bed down the hall to take her to her new room, I had to admit, as much as I liked being postmaster of Ohia, I liked being able to use my Secret Service training too.

Trey walked ahead of us, checking the route for threats. I walked beside the gurney as an orderly pushed it.

"I'm so glad you're here, Kat," Edith said, gazing up at me. Her energy seemed a little better today.

"Me too, Edith." I reached over and squeezed her limp hand. "Me too."

We reached her new room, a corner unit at the end of the hall on the oncology treatment floor. This was an area of the hospital where visitors were discouraged, due to patients' compromised immune systems.

Edith's new accommodation had a view out the window of Kahului Harbor, where a cruise ship lay at anchor. "Five stars," she whispered and coughed. I held a cup of water for her to sip from as the staffer parked and positioned her bed.

"I heard from hospital security downstairs that Josie and Clara are here to see you," I told Edith, as the nurse hung up her IV rack and assorted monitors. "As soon as we have everything checked out on the floor, we'll let them up to see you."

"Oh good." A little color came back into Edith's wan cheeks. "Something to look forward to."

I waited until the staffer left the room. "Edith, I know this is hard to talk about, but I have a bad feeling about Lola and her motives for being in your house. I don't pretend to know all that's gone on between the two of you, but my advice as a friend and a protection professional is that you should change your will."

"You don't mince words, do you?" Edith set her mouth, her bright blue eyes flashing with temper. "No, you don't know what has happened between my daughter and me. How could a young, single woman, without a family, have any idea what we've been through? This is none of your business."

I felt her words like a slap and stepped back from the bed. The neutral expression of my training fell into place, hiding the hurt. "I apologize if my advice offended you." I spun on my heel and stepped outside the room, shutting the door with care.

Trey approached from his physical search of the floor. He was wearing green scrubs and a mask, with a hospital staff ID badge dangling around his neck. He looked the part perfectly. "All clear, Agent Smith."

"Call me Kat," I said. "I'm not working for the agency on this."

"Okay, Kat." Trey pulled down his mask and smiled. He was older than Wakea, with a short red beard that contrasted with salt-and-pepper hair. He radiated the kind of calm competency that was valuable in our field. "Is the client all settled in?"

"Yes. I'm going to fetch her visitors, if you could mind the door."

"No problem." He went inside the room looking like any other hospital employee.

I headed for the stairs. Not only did I want to check that the stairs were empty, but I needed a moment. Once inside the stairwell, I sank onto the top step and wrapped my arms around myself. I squeezed, hard.

I might be a recovering touchphobe, but I knew how to give myself a hug.

And a talking-to. "Come on, Kat. You know better than to take what Edith said personally. She's stressed, in pain, and fighting for her life. And she's correct. It's none of your business. She gets to leave her estate to whoever she chooses. Even if her daughter is a lush, and her granddaughter is an attempted murderer, and both of them are out to dig her an early grave—if she wants to hand them a shovel, that's her right. You said your piece. Now let it go." Gripping my own arms, I shook myself vigorously for good measure. "Get over it."

This probably looked a little like I was having a seizure, because a nurse stepping onto the landing widened her eyes. "Are you all right?"

I grinned and shot to my feet. "Fine! Have a great day!" I took off down the stairs to the bottom floor as fast as my Nikes would carry me. I had visitors to fetch for Edith. That I could do.

21

ANA:

In my new life with Fabio Chang, Saturday was just another day to figure out what we wanted to do—and today we were talking about taking his yacht out for a spin. We were in his SUV, being driven to the Waikiki harbor, when my phone rang.

The only person who had my number was Mom. I answered on speaker so Fabio could listen in; I had no secrets from him. "Hi, Mom."

"Why haven't you called?" she whined.

I grimaced at Fabio. He smiled and looked out the window. "I tried to call yesterday but there was no signal. Where are you?"

"On Maui. In my mother's house."

She'd been drinking, I could tell. "I tried to call because I don't think it's a good idea for you to go to Maui and stir things up with her."

"Edith's not here. She's had a heart attack."

My brows flew up. "Really? That's great news."

"And I guess it's good you're not with me, because that giant woman came over and tried to get me to leave, and then the cops came and did a search for you."

I exhaled gently, holding onto control. "And what did you tell them?"

"That I didn't know where you are. That we had a falling-out."

"Both are true, Mom. You don't know where I am. And you're on your own with whatever you're doing."

"Are you still with that gangster boy toy?"

Fabio smirked and I rolled my eyes. "None of your business."

"That means you're still seeing him. Well, I wouldn't want that information to fall into the wrong hands."

"Mom. Seriously?" I tugged a handful of hair in frustration. "You're blackmailing me now? Don't even try."

She gave a boozy chuckle. "I know. I'm lonely, though. When are you coming over to Maui?"

"We're working on the Edith situation from here. We have things in motion. Sit tight and don't make trouble." I thought of something. "And look for any access codes or hidden records Edith has stashed in the house. We want to find the information she has on New Ohia. Anything she's got squirreled away that could have an impact on the case against the development."

Fabio nodded approvingly, but Mom snorted on her end. "You think I haven't been turning this place inside out? I haven't found anything but a little stash of costume jewelry. You cleaned her out already, Ana. She's got nothing hidden here."

"We'll have to make sure of that," I said. "At some point, we'll connect. Just lie low and be patient, okay?"

"I'll try. I just want a little company. If we were together . . ."

I hung up on her pity party.

Fabio patted my knee sympathetically. "Your mom is a piece of work."

"I know." I rested my chin on my hand and stared unseeingly out the window as we pulled into the harbor and parked.

"This ought to cheer you up." Fabio got out, then came around and opened the door for me. He was so thoughtful that way. It was easy to forget he was a crime lord and not just a hot rich guy. "Come see our boat, the Money Pit."

"Why do you have it if it's such a money pit?"

"That's its name. Money Pit."

I laughed. "Seriously?"

"Technically, the yacht belongs to the family, but I'm the only one who uses it, so I gave it a name that fits."

"I like that about you." I smoothed the white jeans I wore with boat shoes and a scoop neck tee under a navy windbreaker—another box of nice clothes had miraculously appeared on the doorstep of Fabio's mansion that morning. "Should I tell you I've never been on a yacht before? Or any boat, for that matter."

"I was hoping you'd say that."

He led me along the wooden boards of a floating dock past many a watercraft. What types they were escaped me—but the one we stopped in front of? Even I could tell the gleaming white palace was a yacht. "Wow."

"And I get to use it whenever I want." Fabio pointed me to a gangplank where two men in uniform stood waiting. "After you."

I shut my eyes for a second before stepping onto the yacht. I was suspicious of anything that seemed too good to be true, and this detour into a fairy tale qualified.

Fabio touched my back. "It's real," he whispered in my ear. "And I want you here."

I stepped onto the deck, and let my heart open a little bit more. Might as well enjoy the dream while it lasted.

22

I PASSED by the hospital's security guy, Hank, and waved. Josie and Clara were waiting in the entrance lobby of the hospital, seated on a molded plastic bench against the wall and looking none too happy about it.

Clara jumped to her feet at the sight of me, a gorgeous, flowing caftan swirling as she stood. Josie, dressed in a Hawaiian print muumuu, got up more slowly, propping herself on her O_2 tank. Both of their smiles were bright. "So good to see you, Kat!" Josie exclaimed.

The angst I'd been struggling with since Edith barked at me slipped away as I greeted the women in their red hats. Clara wore a scarlet boater, and Josie wore a dyed coconut frond creation trimmed with a feather band.

"So glad you two could make it out to see Edith today. I think she could use a mood booster," I said.

"We came bearing gifts." Clara gestured to a cloth bag she carried. "I have a crochet project for her to work on while she's here."

"And I brought a thermos of noni tea." Josie patted a metal container she'd slipped into the wheeled wire carrier that held her portable oxygen tank. "This will speed her recovery." Josie had schooled me on the many uses of the native plant in an unforgettable lesson behind my shack.

"Great," I said. "I'm helping with security while Edith's laid up." I didn't tell them about the recent attempted breach on Edith's room. Why worry them further? "I'm sorry about the hassle waiting to see her—but you're some of the only people allowed on her floor and we had to make an exception for you. I'll explain more while we're on the elevator." The ladies followed me across the lobby and into the elevator.

"Opal sent some of Artie's coffeecake," Clara said, holding open her fabric satchel for me to see the wrapped squares. "And Pearl didn't want to be left out, so she sent along a packet of dried squid," Josie said, opening a lidded basket she held.

I leaned over to look, and a waft of potent fishy smell hit my nose. The scent increased as the elevator doors closed.

"Phew! Does she make that herself?" I peered at crusty, curled-up dried tentacles wrapped in cheerful yellow cellophane and secured with a beaded bow. "I mean, the presentation is lovely, but . . ."

"Her cousin catches the squid on his fishing boat. She does prepare it herself. It's a bit of an acquired taste," Josie said.

"Like noni, then," I replied, smiling.

"Like noni," Josie echoed.

"Well she might have to wait to dine on that until out of the oncology ward. They prohibit strong smells on the floor due to triggering ill patients." I hit the STOP button on the elevator. "Listen, ladies. While I have you to myself. Without going into too much detail, I need to let you know that the threat on Edith's life is real. As soon as possible, we need to get her out of the hospital to somewhere safer and more defensible. Do you know where she could be moved?"

"Yes," Clara said. "We've already been working on it. We have another Red Hat friend who owns a mansion in Wailuku with a wall around it and heavy security—she has a lot of priceless art and antiquities. She's agreed to let Edith stay with her once she's discharged."

"That's terrific!" I exclaimed.

"It's near the hospital, too, in case she needs follow-up care," Clara said.

"Can you give me your friend's contact info? I'll have to talk with her about security before Edith is moved onto the premises."

Clara sent me the contact details for a woman named Beth Krieger, and I stored them in my phone.

"Okay, thanks. Another thing," I continued. "I have concerns about Lola and Ana, and their motives around Edith's estate. I asked her to change her will, but Edith told me to mind my own business. In no uncertain terms."

Josie shook her head gently. "She would do that."

"Yes, and normally that would be fine, but I have a bad feeling about those two. Even if Lola means Edith no harm, Ana actively hates her and tried to kill her on Oahu. We think Ana might be involved with a hit the Changs have out on Edith." I told the ladies a bit more about what Sophie had discovered. "I can't say anything more to Edith on the subject, but perhaps one of you could put in a word?"

"I will," Josie said stoutly. "I understand wanting to leave a legacy for your offspring—I have five children myself. But Edith could put her estate in trust or something. Remove the incentive for them to . . . to . . ." She crumpled suddenly, covering her face with her hands.

"I'm sorry." I patted Josie's shoulder as Clara tsked, fussing to get a tissue. "I hate to bring up these heavy topics, but here we are. Maybe a therapist could help?"

"Does the hospital have a social worker?" Clara asked.

I nodded with relief. "I'm sure they do. I'll figure out who that is and send them to the room to meet with you, if they're available. I think it's standard operating procedure for elderly patients to have a meeting before discharge, anyway." I hit the button again and the elevator lurched upward. I pasted a smile on my face. "I'm sure everything's going to be fine."

Josie sniffed into her tissue, and Clara watched the numbers change over the door. I hadn't reassured anyone, not even myself. I left them at Edith's room with a heavy heart as I went in search of the hospital's social worker. After finding her, verifying her identity, and passing her through security to join Edith and her friends, I headed to the parking lot and unlocked the new-to-me, white Ford Explorer.

"I think I'll call you Great White Shark," I said aloud and patted the dash. "Sharkey for short. I hope this is the beginning of a beautiful friendship." Sharkey roared to life in answer as I pushed the ignition button, and I revved the engine just for fun. "Let's go find Beth Krieger's house and check the security there, now that we know Edith's scheduled for discharge tomorrow." I thumbed to the address in my phone's GPS and was pleased to see that it was automatically hooked up and displayed directions to the destination on the dashboard screen. "Gotta say I'm loving the modern technology after driving Josie's van the last few days."

Sharkey put on my Classic Rock playlist in reply, and we pulled out of the parking lot to "I Love Rock 'n' Roll" by Joan Jett. It felt like a dialogue with a new friend, and I hoped it was as I patted the dash. "Take me to Beth Krieger's house, Sharkey."

23

As Clara had mentioned, the neighborhood of Wailuku Heights was not far from the hospital, and I was soon turning into a landscaped area that commanded a view of the island and Haleakala in the distance. Beth Krieger's house was at the highest point of a development of custom homes. When I arrived at a hammered copper gate topped with decorative spikes, I smiled. "This is a good start."

I pushed the ADMIT button on a curved black kiosk with a blank video screen. "Hello? This is Kat Smith with Security Solutions. I have an appointment." I liked how that new job sounded when I said it.

"Hi, Kat." The blank screen bloomed into a video feed that showed a smiling woman's face topped by a scarlet bowler. "Where's your red hat? The girls told me you were one of us."

"I'm an honorary member. I'm postmaster of Ohia, so I have to maintain color neutrality," I said.

"You're already wearing several hats, then." Ms. Krieger chuckled at her own joke. "Come on in." The screen went blank and the gate, wrapped in artfully disguised steel reinforcement rods to prevent any sort of ramming, trundled open.

I drove forward between a pair of trees trained to arch over the driveway, each of them covered in purple orchid blossoms. I took my time navigating past a kidney-shaped koi pond surrounded by ferns and filled by a small waterfall. A curving path wound between flower terraces and paralleled the driveway. I eventually passed a garage with three closed doors to park at the top of a roundabout in front of the Krieger mansion. I hit the lock on Sharkey as I exited, but that was probably overkill. Who would break into my humble vehicle in this over-the-top Shangri-La?

A set of flagstone steps led to a pair of red-lacquered double doors. I didn't have time to knock or ring before they opened inward automatically with a gentle sigh of hydraulics, admitting me to a grand foyer topped by a stained-glass cupola.

"Wow, Ms. Krieger," I told the woman approaching me across a sea of black marble floor. "Your home is splendiferous."

"Please, call me Beth. I'm thankful to have a place that can provide Edith some protection." Beth was freckle-faced and pleasantly rounded. She wore a tee and capri pants in colors that set off her red hat, and as she reached me, she slid an arm through mine in a friendly gesture that made me stiffen. She didn't notice my touchphobia and gave a gentle tug. "Let me show you around so we can make sure everything's ready for Edith's arrival."

I detached myself as anxiety prickled the skin all over my body. "Thanks again for your hospitality. Where's the room you have picked out for Edith? Let's start there."

Beth spoke over her shoulder as she set off down a hall to the left of the entryway. "I thought the garden room would be perfect for her recovery. Right this way."

Several closed doors led off the hall, and the opposite wall was glass, facing an interior courtyard. A fountain featuring stone dolphins was set off by a view of the deep green, sculptured West Maui Mountains.

Beth opened a door at the end of the hall. "Here we are."

I couldn't suppress a gasp. The bedroom she intended for Edith had one of those huge corner windows with no seam that over-looked an abundantly blooming rose garden. The garden was positioned to lead the eye toward the walls of a steep green mountain currently shrouded in poufy clouds.

I had to tear my gaze away from the view to assess the room itself. Walls painted a pink so soft it reminded me of dawn's fragile glow surrounded a four-poster bed decked in creamy linens and hung about with gauze curtains. Beside the bed, a table with a crystal lamp was stocked with mystery novels, and in the corner a chaise upholstered in pink velvet invited lounging and reading when not gazing out the window.

"Can I move in here?" I cupped my cheeks in delight as I surveyed this girly-girl fantasy.

Beth clapped with pleasure. "Isn't it lovely for someone recovering from surgery?"

"It's lovely for anyone." I approached the corner window and touched the material. "What's this window made of?"

"Polycarbonate and Plexiglas. It's shatterproof."

"That's good." The earth outside was close, though, since the house was built on a slope. "Unfortunately, we'll need to screen Edith from anyone being able to see inside."

"No problem." Beth pulled a cord on drapes that were drawn back, and a transparent film moved across the window. "No one can see in, but she can still see out. The other layer of curtains are blackouts for nighttime."

"Perfect." I walked into the adjoining bathroom. The rose luxury theme continued, but the window in here was too high and small to allow any entrance. The door was also heavy and featured a bolt style lock. "This bathroom could be Edith's safe room, should she need one. Solid construction and this lock would be hard to get past." I turned to a walk-in shower stall made of translucent glass bricks. An antique, deep, claw-foot tub was set against one wall. "These are handy for taking cover in."

"That's not the usual comment people make when they see that

tub," Beth chuckled. "But I can see you know your security stuff. I'd
hate to think Edith would ever need such a thing, especially when
we have a real safe room in the house and a pretty sophisticated
alarm system. Come and I'll show you the command center, as my
husband calls it."

I exited the room with one last, longing gaze at the view and
followed Beth back toward the entrance. We entered a living room
with sliders that faced the courtyard and mountains. I didn't have
time to gawk as Beth led me to a big-screen TV.

"Over here." She pressed a decorative divot in the wood frame
surrounding it. The panel that the TV was mounted on opened
soundlessly. Lights bloomed on inside a hidden room behind it.
"This is our safe room and the house's command center. It's bullet-
and fireproof and has its own dedicated communication and power
lines."

We stepped into a cool, tidy space. One wall was stacked with
square water bottles and a shelf of food supplies. A mini bath and
shower combo occupied a corner, and bunk beds took up another
wall. A third side was given to a long desk with two chairs. Monitors
featured ever-changing views of the house, and a console equipped
with a keyboard gave a clue as to the security functions. A final wall
was devoted to a comfy-looking couch that faced a TV on a stand
with more books stacked underneath.

"You've thought of everything." I put my hands on my hips and
did a three-sixty to take it all in. "This is . . . impressive."

Beth shrugged. "My husband worked in digital security. He
loves all that end of the world, zombie apocalypse stuff."

"And you?"

"I'm a programmer." She adjusted her bright bowler and
smiled. "We're geeks together. It works."

"This is way more security than we could ever hope to set up for
Edith. Thanks for your hospitality."

"Anything for a fellow Red Hat! I've been wanting to get to

know Edith, but she's so busy all the time. This is my chance to have her to myself." Beth's hazel eyes sparkled.

"One last question. Do you have any security staff, or do you run all this yourself?"

"Ourselves, with the help of our house." She clapped her hands. "Fantasia! Music please. And deactivate the gate—our guest will be leaving soon."

"You got it, Beth." The voice that came out of some hidden speaker had a distinct Polynesian cadence to it.

"Your smart house is named Fantasia? Nice." I smiled and followed Beth out of the safe room. "Well, we'll be sending some staffers from Security Solutions to help while Edith's here. I hope that's not an issue. Do you have room here for them to stay?"

"The more the merrier," Beth said. "Our kids are grown and gone, so we have extra rooms. Come on back to the living room and feast your eyes on our view before you get on the road."

I did and was delighted by the way the evening light slanted from the west and lit the clouds snagged on the tops of the mountains. "Does this ever get old?"

"Something would be wrong with us if it did," Beth said, and I liked her even more.

24

SUNDAY DAWNED with a full agenda planned. I spent the night at Lei's again, but this time we all stayed sober and went to bed early. A good thing, because there was a lot to do to get ready for Edith's planned discharge from the hospital to Beth's house.

I started the day with a quick strategy session at the Security Solutions office in Wailuku. Sophie joined on video along with my two main guys, Chance and Trey, and the two additional staffers Sophie deployed from Oahu to complete Edith's detail.

"The trickiest part will be moving Edith, code named Eagle, from the hospital to her new digs at the Kriegers' house," I told the team, two of whom were still guarding our client and attending via video. "A private ambulance service is scheduled to do the transport. Edith will be taken directly to the ambulance bay, where we will be waiting. I will be riding with her, and Chance and Trey will be following." I made eye contact with Chance. "Make sure to take the signage off your SUV. Everyone in scrubs and masks. We don't want to draw any attention to ourselves."

"Yes ma'am," Chance said.

"Just Kat, please. Now, did Sophie issue you radios and

earpieces?" We got all of that sorted, synchronized our timepieces and schedule, and left to move "Eagle" to her new nest.

"I wish Edith was feeling better. She'd get such a kick out of being called 'Eagle' and all of the arrangements we're making," I said as I drove with Trey in my SUV the short distance to the hospital.

"She's pretty sharp for someone who recently had a heart attack," Trey said, stroking his short red beard. "I've been giving her reports on our plans as they developed. You're right, she's interested in everything. She must be a real dynamo when she's operating at full capacity."

"You have no idea," I said, thinking back to when we spent a weekend together at the Bishop Museum on Oahu and evaded another attempt on Edith's life.

I parked near the ambulance bay, and we hopped out to join the rest of the team for the transfer.

THE MOVE to Beth's house was uneventful—which in security terms is a success. Edith was wiped out by the process, though, and as soon as she was settled, she fell asleep in the rose room with the drapes pulled.

I met with the security team in Fantasia's living room to go over schedules and procedures going forward. After that, Beth's husband, a stocky man named Arnold with a bald head and bright green eyes, led the operatives two at a time to check out the command center and tour the house and grounds. Two agents would be on hand at the estate twenty-four seven, but they'd be rotating in and out, so all needed to be familiar with Fantasia's many features and layout.

"A little bird told me this was your beverage of choice," our hostess said, handing me a tall, frosty mug of root beer.

"Thank you, Beth." I gratefully accepted the beverage. "I'm glad 'Eagle' is officially nested somewhere safe and comfortable."

"Are you staying with us too? Because I've got a special room you'd love." Beth acted like she wanted more people in her house.

I grimaced. "Unfortunately, no. I am the postmaster in Ohia and currently the sole employee, so I have to get back out there this afternoon. I need to be ready for work tomorrow." I drained the delicious bubbly beverage and handed Beth the mug. "If Edith's still here by Friday, I should come out and spend the weekend. Relieve one of the guys."

"I don't know why she wouldn't still be here," Beth said. "She shouldn't go home until the threat has passed, and I heard her daughter is at her place and may cause trouble."

In the hullabaloo, Lola occupying Edith's house had slipped my mind. "As soon as Edith is strong enough, we'll need to assess the situation," I said. "You can reach me during the day at the post office."

"No hurry or pressure. You're welcome anytime, Kat," she said.

I handed Trey my earpiece and radio, made sure he had everything he needed to be in charge in my absence, and said my goodbyes.

But I couldn't leave without peeking in at my protectee. I pressed the lever-style handle of the bedroom door and moved it gently open.

Edith's face was turned away, her white hair soft and fluffy as goosedown against the pale pink pillow. Her gentle snores, familiar to me from our other trip, filled the room.

"Rest well, dear friend," I whispered, a twinge tightening my chest. Though I'd interacted with Edith during the transition, and Josie had told me the social worker's visit was "helpful" without any detail of what that meant, the two of us still needed to get past the conflict that had arisen when I asked her to change her will.

I shut the door as gently as I'd opened it.

Trey carried a comfy-looking chair over and set it beside the bedroom door. He took a seat and cracked open one of the many mystery books lying around the house. "She'll be fine," he told me. "I'll make sure she's safe."

"Of course." I straightened my back and erased whatever sentimental expression I'd worn. "Let me know if anything comes up."

"You got it, Kat."

There was nothing left to do but go. I waved goodbye to Beth as I drove Sharkey through the turnaround and out of the estate. The name Fantasia was woven in ironwork vines that wrapped the gate, visible only on exit. "What a place," I murmured aloud. I'd seen a lot of rich people's homes but the combination of beauty, security, comfort, and function that made up Beth and Arnold's estate was unique.

After a short stop at the Maui Police Department to brief Lei and Pono on the setup at Fantasia and check if there was anything new on the case (there wasn't), I got on the road for Hana. I planned to stop in at Edith's first thing after the two-hour drive.

I didn't put on music as I drove through the bustling town of Kahului, preferring to go over a mental checklist of the security protocols we'd put in place, along with a mental map I'd memorized of the estate.

As I mulled, I drove along the island's stunning eastern coastline overlooking the ocean. Palms waved. Surfers played. The water was the color of good Arizona turquoise. I passed a well-known beach called Hoʻokipa, where prevailing brisk winds held up kiteboarders flitting like brightly colored butterflies over the sea.

I couldn't think of anything I'd left undone, but my distraction ended with a fizz of alarm when I spotted a tail in my rearview mirror—and it wasn't a peacock tail, cattail, or comet tail. This tail was a big black SUV with mirrored windows and a bad vibe etched on its aggressive chrome grille.

I knew a drug lord vehicle when I saw one.

25

MAYBE THE ENORMOUS black SUV wasn't after me. Maybe this classic gangsta-mobile was out for a leisurely drive to Hana, and the mirrored windows that violated vehicle safety code were so the sweet family inside could enjoy privacy. Or, maybe they were movie stars enjoying paradise and hiding from paparazzi.

But I couldn't take that risk. The vehicle had stuck with me for too many turns, and now we funneled onto the super narrow, precipitous, and always picturesque road to Hana. There wouldn't be a way to find out what they were up to until I tried to give them the slip.

I speeded up, hoping to lose the Big Black Behemoth (BBB for short.) I put Sharkey in Sport Mode and zipped around a dawdling tourist vehicle that had pulled over to take a photo of a waterfall—usually the most dangerous moment of any drive on this route. The BBB stuck with me, accelerating around the car, and causing a tourist with a phone camera to lose her hat in the gust of its passing.

I scowled at the vehicle looming in my rearview. BBB could still be an impatient Hana resident, trying to make time on the way home. I leaned forward and adjusted my mirrors for a tighter angle, quickly memorizing the license plate. "Okay, Sharkey. Hope you had a recent tune-up, 'cause things are about to get interesting."

I punched the accelerator and zoomed forward, zigging and zagging along the narrow road using driving techniques I'd practiced for months on a professional course. Yeah, horns screamed, people scattered, and chickens flew up in the air, but by golly I was outpacing that SUV.

I managed to get ahead by several curves in the road, mainly because the Ford Explorer was a smaller, nimbler vehicle than the BBB—but as soon as we hit a little straightaway, the monster easily caught up. I had no further doubt as to the driver's intentions when that ugly chrome grille smacked Sharkey's bumper, hard. "Oh, son of a salamander!"

Sharkey's tires screeched as we went into a spin—and that's not a good thing on the road to Hana. Many parts of the famous route are tricky to navigate, and this section was one of them, with a ditch on one side and a cliff on the other, and no shoulder anywhere in-between.

"Crumb cakes!" I managed to keep two wheels on the road and swing the vehicle around, swiping the edge of a drop-off hundreds of feet to the ocean as we spun—but then I landed in the watery ditch with a solid crunch and a big white airbag punch to the face.

If you've ever had your airbag deploy, it's not a pain-free experience. For a long moment I was pretty sure I was knocked out. And then I blinked. Alive, but stunned. Blinked more. Nope. Still blind.

The airbag was plastered against my face and body, doing its job and holding me back against the seat. As the thing deflated, I could see again. "Whew. Thank goodness." I shoved the smothering white fabric away and did a quick damage assessment.

Sharkey's hood was dug into the red dirt of the ditch, and we were at a steep angle. The smell of burnt rubber competed with that of powder from the airbag. The ticking of the hot engine filled my ears. But other than whatever bruising I'd received from the seatbelt around my chest and the airbag squashed into my face, I was unhurt.

I tried the door handle—nothing happened. I pressed the button to roll down the window by instinct. The accessories were still on though the engine had stalled. But the window showed me that I was inches away from the red dirt and black lava stone cliff rising above the ditch. Nope, getting out on the driver's side wasn't going to happen. The door was pinned shut.

Would the BBB come back and make another run at me? Or had they moved on? Either way, I was a turtle with its feet in the air —helpless. I got the belt off and located my backpack on the floor beside me. I fumbled through it to remove my weapon. Once I had my gun available, I felt more in control of whatever came next.

I pushed and shoved the clinging material of the airbag out of the way and crawled out of my seat over to the passenger side, which was at an uphill angle, but doable to exit. I grabbed my backpack and the keys, then moved to the passenger door. It was no small feat to shove the door almost straight up with no leverage and gravity against me, but all those push-ups made it possible.

I got the door open enough to peek out. No passersby came to my aid, though I could hear the swish of tires going past, because the SUV had spun in a circle and now faced toward oncoming traffic. The vehicle was neatly inserted into the ditch and tucked behind a large bush that blocked any view of Sharkey from approaching vehicles. "Son of a toad. Isn't this grand."

On the plus side, though, there was no sign of the BBB. I was likely out of danger for the moment.

How long had the vehicle been following me?

Where had they picked me up?

Most importantly, had they seen me exit Fantasia's grounds?

Those questions gave me a chill.

As I crawled out and turned to study the damage to Sharkey, which seemed pretty minimal considering, I pondered what the driver of the BBB might know. I hadn't noticed the vehicle until I was past the town of Paia and on the unruly part of the road as it left civilization. Even so, it was possible they'd picked me up as early as the hospital and now knew where Edith was.

"But I bet they picked me up at the police station. Maybe there's a mole in the department that spotted me talking to Lei and Pono and had me followed," I muttered. "I had you less than one day, Sharkey. I'm sorry."

I turned away from my recently acquired wheels with regret and pushed through the branches of the concealing bush. I got myself out onto what passed as the shoulder of the road and shook out my limbs, rotated my neck. Everything still worked, though my nerves were jangled. I dug in the backpack for my phone and held it up.

No Service.

"Heckfire! Can't a girl get a break?"

I took a moment to stretch my limbs again. There was nothing to do but start walking, and hope I came to somewhere with signal soon.

26

I CONSIDERED HITCHHIKING as tourist cars whizzed past and I worried about being spanked by a side mirror—but my nerves were so frazzled from the car chase and wipeout that I didn't want to have to talk to anyone. I'd have to explain how I came to be walking on the side of the road with airbag dust all over me. I'd stick my thumb out when I was ready to deal with people.

My pulse gradually settled as I strode along, thankful I always wore clothing for movement and my beloved Nikes made for walking. My nose and the area around my eyes began to swell from the collision between my face and the airbag. Breathing too deep hurt because that darn seatbelt had squashed my chest. Still, I'd have been injured a lot worse without those safety devices, and I knew it.

"I hope Sharkey isn't too damaged. I've had that car one day. ONE DAY!" That crisped my bacon more than anything that had happened so far. I'd enjoyed having my own set of wheels for the first time since I arrived on Maui. But Sharkey ending up in a ditch wasn't the worst thing that had happened with this little disaster. Not being able to communicate and reach my team to tell them that someone might know Edith's location was the terrifying thing.

Every few feet I held up my phone and checked for bars. "Nada.

Zilch. Big fat zero. How can this be the modern age?" There was no reply except the squawk of a mynah disturbed from picking at a squashed guava in the road as I came too close.

I noticed my surroundings as I found my long-distance walking stride. The deep blue heaven overhead was filled with white cloud galleons moving briskly in the trade winds. Off the jungled shoulder, the ocean sparkled far below the green cliffs of the road I walked. Small waterfalls every hundred yards or so tumbled down the erosion-sculpted bluffs, each one unique and surrounded by trembling maidenhair ferns, velvety moss, and tiny wild purple orchids. Here and there in the wet areas, toads hopped on the road. Big ones, the size of my hand, all brown and warty, sitting near the edges of the asphalt or as flat as amphibian pancakes from passing cars.

"Gross," I muttered, and then spotted another of the hapless critters hopping awkwardly onto the tarmac, right into the path of an oncoming vehicle.

"Stop!" I jumped out from the shoulder, waving my arms. The driver slammed on the brakes. I grabbed a stick and herded the toad safely into the ditch (the same one Sharkey rested in a mile or so back.)

The car that came to a halt was a Honda CRV, and the woman who rolled down the window and stuck her head out was Pua Chang. Sunshine gleamed on her shiny black bob and her eyes were hidden behind huge round sunglasses. "Kat? What are you doing here?"

"Long story." Pua had been a thorn in my side and a conflicted ally at different times; our relationship was complicated. "Can I get a ride to somewhere with signal?"

"Of course."

I got into her car. As I drew my long legs in and set my muddy Nikes on her pristine floor mat, all the aches and pains I'd been keeping at bay with worry and movement flooded over me. Tears prickled my eyes. I fumbled with the seatbelt and pulled it gingerly across my bruised midsection.

"I was in an accident. My car is in a ditch a mile or so back. I need a tow truck and possibly medical assistance."

"Oh, no!" Pua's pretty face scrunched up in distress as she removed her sunglasses to check me over. Of course, she was perfectly made up and wearing a crisp white sleeveless blouse and flowered capri pants. Cork-heeled sandals in pale blue decorated her pedicured little feet. "Let's get you to the urgent care! They're the closest place with a signal. I know from experience."

My former postal clerk, out on bail pending her case for attempted murder and drug-running, put the Honda in gear. She pulled out in front of a tourist vehicle, honking like a New York driver on vacation. I gripped the armrests as Pua drove Nascar-style toward Hana.

"Thanks for the ride," I said through clenched teeth as we zipped across the curve around a bluff. She clearly had the whole route memorized.

"Need some water? I have a fresh bottle in the holder on the side door." Of course she did, just in case she had a passenger who was thirsty. This woman thought of everything.

"Thank you." I helped myself to the water bottle, chugging it down with a couple of Tylenol from my backpack.

We pulled up in front of the Hana Health Urgent Care building in record time. I got out, pulling my backpack after me. "Thanks for the ride, Pua."

She didn't drive away. Instead, she turned off the car and got out, circling around the front. "Kat, let me help."

Maybe she was willing to help me with something bigger than getting a ride to the urgent care. Maybe she was willing to help me with the Chang hit on Edith. But I'd have to take a gamble in telling her, and that was scary. "Can I trust you to help with a bigger, more serious situation? A matter of life and death?"

Pua's eyes widened, then narrowed. "That's not a fair question without being able to know more. Circumstances have put us on opposite sides of an issue more than once."

That was an understatement!

"Okay. I have a big crisis going on and it involves your family. Would you be willing to help me? I'd make sure the cops know you've been cooperating."

"If it's about New Ohia, I've already tried to help with that." Pua fiddled with her cute little raffia purse. "Is it something different?"

"Yes. Though it may be related."

"Let's go check in and you can make your phone calls and get medical treatment. I'll stay with you and think about it. You shouldn't be going through this alone, in any case."

My chest hurt. The sun was beating on my head and making me dizzy. I still had a mountain of communication to get through, and her request was reasonable. "That's kind of you."

We must have looked like an odd couple as we walked up the stone steps of the urgent care building together. We couldn't be more opposite physically, circumstantially, and in personality. Yet I felt a connection with this woman. I'd trusted that connection before, and it had worked out. I'd trust it again if she'd agree to help —and the stakes really were life and death.

27

PUA WAITED OUTSIDE as I was examined in the Hana Health Urgent Care. "Just some bruises," the nurse practitioner said as she handed me a prescription for mild pain meds. "The chest is going to take a while to heal, and that bruise will be painful. Your face will take a bit to settle as well. If you develop whiplash symptoms in the next few days, come on back. We'll do our best to treat you and document for insurance, then set you up with some physical therapy."

The last thing I wanted to do was try to find my way back to Hana for some painful PT while my wheels were in the shop. And insurance, health or otherwise? I had no idea what was going on with that for me. Which reminded me of all the phone calls I had to make, beginning with Sophie and then a tow truck.

"Thanks. I gotta go." I slid off the table and hurried out the door, already on the phone to my new boss. I slipped into the restroom so I could have privacy, and briefed Sophie from my perch on the porcelain throne. "It's possible Edith's location is compromised. Everyone needs to be on high alert," I said, wrapping up the spate of words it took to get Sophie up to speed. "I got a plate number on the Big Black Behemoth that ran me off the road. It would be great if you could call it in to Lei since I've got to contact a tow truck. Speaking of, does the car have insurance?"

"Of course. All our vehicles have full coverage, and we have additional employee health and hazard insurance. Your medical expenses will be fully covered. I'll get our Human Resources department working on a compensation claim for you." Sophie said. "I'm so sorry this happened, Kat, but I'm glad you're working for us, and we can take care of you."

"Me too." I rubbed my sore chest gingerly. "In a weird twist, Pua Chang picked me up on the side of the road. She's doing a good job acting like she cares. I plan to ask her about who might be behind the hit on Edith."

A long pause. I could hear Sophie thinking, see her elegant brows drawn together in my mind's eye. "Seems like you might be taking a risk. Can you trust her?"

"She's a Chang, but she seems to want to do the right thing," I said. "The information she's given me before was good."

"Then by all means, attempt rapprochement," Sophie said.

I would have to look up that French-sounding word when I had time, but I wasn't about to admit it. "Okay. I better call that tow truck next."

"No. I'll handle that for you." I heard the rapid clickety-clack of her fingers on computer keys. "You get home and rest. It's been a big day. I'll get you status reports from the Eagle Team and on the vehicle as soon as I have them. I'll ask Lei to check on the plate and put in a police report for your accident. We've got to document everything."

"Thanks so much." I was glad I was sitting; I felt a little dizzy with relief I wasn't going to have to deal with my poor, abused Sharkey for the moment. I gave her the BBB's license plate number. "I'll ask Pua for a ride home and talk to her then."

"Perfect. Let's touch base tomorrow." Sophie ended the call.

I got up off the toilet and washed my face and hands. The aches and pains of today's adventure seemed to be amplifying by the minute.

Pua was perusing a dog-eared People magazine in the waiting area. She sprang to her feet when she saw me. "What did they say about your injuries?" She genuinely seemed to care.

"Nothing some rest and aspirin won't cure," I said with forced cheerfulness. "Would you mind giving me a ride home?"

"Of course. It's on my way." She opened the door, and then hovered around as I lumbered out of the building, a hummingbird to my stork. At the car, she opened the passenger side door and held it for me. I resisted the urge to roll my eyes and said, "thank you," instead.

Once we were en route, I cleared my throat. "Pua. I'd like to ask you something."

She glanced my way. "Do you need anything at Hasegawa's before we leave town? I have to stop and pick up a few things."

Hasegawa's had more foodstuffs than Artie and Opal carried. I mentally summoned the negligible contents of my tiny fridge at the shack. "Actually, I need a resupply as well."

We pulled into the store near the end of Hana town. Bigger than Opal and Artie's, the market held a little of everything from rain boots to bestselling books. I filled a basket with foodstuffs and a bag of lychees. I also procured a catnip mouse for Tiki—she might enjoy disemboweling the stuffed toy.

Pua picked up what she needed, too.

Back in the car, I tried again. "I have to ask you something. Do you know anything about who's behind the attacks on Edith?"

She frowned. "I heard it was her granddaughter, Ana. That girl is rotten."

"There's more to it. Ana is still on the loose, so she could be involved, but a man disguised as a nurse tried to kill Edith at the hospital, and now I've been run off the road intentionally. Rumor has it the Changs are trying to neutralize Edith, so she won't be around to organize resistance to New Ohia."

Pua wasn't the type to slam on the brakes. She put her blinker on and eased off the road into the food truck parking area instead. "I think we should get something to eat before this conversation."

"Okay." I took this as a sign she was willing to talk, and my stomach rumbled loudly in agreement.

As we settled at a picnic table, carrying takeout containers holding a traditional Hawaii "plate lunch" of kalua pork on cabbage, macaroni salad, and a couple of scoops of white rice, I remembered I'd promised to update Mr. K on any incidents involving mayhem and danger. Thankfully, there were a few bars of signal here. "Excuse me, Pua. I have to make a quick call."

I got up, walked far enough away that Pua couldn't hear, and phoned Keone. He didn't answer, which was a bit of a relief because I could leave a message about recent happenings and that I was okay. Relationship requirements fulfilled, I returned to the table and sat, opening my box of food. I dug into my meal and shoveled it in rapidly. Pua ate in silence as well.

"I think we should reach out to Terence Chang," Pua said abruptly, closing her container.

"Who's Terence Chang?"

"He's the legit Big Island head of the family."

I met her dark brown eyes. "Legit? What do you mean?"

"He's clean. He used to be in the life, but isn't anymore."

"Why is he a good person to talk to?"

"Terence is in charge. He knows all the players and operations. He's been known to flip on rogue factions in the family for the better good of everyone. This could be one of those situations. I trust him."

"Then by all means, let's call him."

She took out her phone and pressed a number. The device toned as I tidied up our empty food containers.

I was about to speak with the head of Hawaii's biggest crime family at a picnic table outside of a food truck.

28

In all the scenarios I imagined when I woke up this long-ago Sunday morning, talking on speakerphone at a picnic table to the "legit" head of the Chang crime family wasn't one of them. But here Pua and I were, hunched over her phone with mynahs squawking in the background.

"It's been a while since I heard from you, Auntie Pua." Terence Chang sounded young. His use of the cultural honorific "auntie" confirmed that. "How's your legal situation going?"

Of course, he must know of Pua's pending trial. She brushed that aside. "Thanks for asking, Terence. We can catch up on that another time. I've got you on speaker and I'm calling on another matter. I have someone with me I'd like you to meet. Her name is Kat Smith, and she's the new postmaster in Ohia."

A brief pause while he digested this. "Hello, Ms. Smith. I've heard of you."

"Call me Kat, thanks." I shouldn't have felt flattered that he knew of me when the reasons couldn't be good. "I appreciate an opportunity to talk with you about a matter of life and death."

He snorted. "The things I deal with often are. Auntie Pua, why don't you fill me in?"

I'd been put in my place.

A car with customers arrived. Pua got up. "Let's go to the car where we can have more privacy."

I tossed the rubbish and got into the CRV as Pua got settled, putting the phone in a holder. I shut the door and bit my tongue.

Pua picked up the conversational ball. "Terence, I'm sure you're aware of the situation with the development in New Ohia. There's an active FBI and police investigation into the corporation building the luxury community. I spearheaded the development early on, to provide a place for our family to return to our roots."

All of this Pua had told me. Clearly Terence knew it too as he said, "I'm familiar. Go on, Auntie."

"Kat believes there's a hit out on Edith Pepperwhite, the attorney that's been organizing legal resistance to New Ohia. I called you when I was first arrested to tell you I thought someone in power at the New Ohia Vision, Inc. was going rogue with the project. I stopped getting any communication about the development, and sales are ongoing to outsiders when we all knew that endgame was supposed to be—" she spared me an embarrassed glance, "confined to cash purchases by family and our connections. That was our original mission."

"Yes. I have a lot there myself," Terence said coolly.

I stroked my chin. This part was news to me.

Pua went on. "Things went awry even before Jimmy Ching, the first project manager, was killed. Someone in the corporation is out to make a profit on New Ohia and doesn't care who buys or gets hurt by the scam. Another body, especially that of a highly visible, popular person like Edith, would only draw more attention from authorities."

I was astonished Pua was letting me hear her talk like this—like a connected criminal. I wasn't the only one taking a risk and trusting in our fragile relationship.

"I know who's behind it," Terence said. "I've been staying out of his business there because I figured the feds would shut New Ohia down eventually and that would take care of the situation. I wasn't aware of a hit on Pepperwhite, though. I agree that's going to make our family a target. I'll make some calls."

Both of us sagged in our seats with relief.

"Thanks, Terence. Ohia is my home, and I wanted it to be a place all of our family could enjoy," Pua said. "It's special—the town where the Changs first got established in Hawaii, and the place where we return to be buried. I never would have helped initiate the land deal that began the development if I'd known how badly things would go. Do you think there's any way we can get New Ohia back on track?"

"Seems unlikely with the investigation uncovering so many illegalities," Terence said. "We might need to walk away from this one. I'll call you when I know more." The abrupt buzz of a dial tone told us he was gone.

Pua pressed the End button on her phone and covered her face with her hands.

After a long moment, I gave in to impulse and touched her shoulder. "I'm sorry, Pua. It seems like you meant well." Even if the whole thing had been an attempt to cater to a crime family, which I didn't appreciate.

"I love Ohia," Pua said, her voice muffled by her hands. "I feel responsible for what's happened at the New Ohia development. The people who've died."

I had no response. Since she admitted she'd orchestrated the New Ohia land deal, she was responsible for a lot of the trouble that had come to our little village through the resort development and the murders it had triggered. "When is your trial? I'm happy to be a witness about how you've tried to help fix this mess. Give your attorney my name."

"I don't know if that will help, but thanks." Pua lowered her hands. Her eyes were wet and puffy, her makeup smeared. "And I'm worried for Edith. She's a friend, and if one of my relatives has anything to do with her death . . ." She trailed off.

I dug in the side pocket of the passenger door, found a tissue packet, and handed it to her.

Pua pulled out several soft white squares and blotted her eyes. "The family counts on Terence to keep members in line, even when it means someone has to be disciplined or handed over to the authorities."

I said nothing.

"I'm hoping you won't inform the investigators about this conversation," Pua said, facing me. "Terence needs to be free to do what he does, or I can't imagine how bad things could get."

"I agree it would be bad form for me to share his name and involvement with anyone in law enforcement," I said.

"You don't need to. He has his own relationships with the cops," Pua said. "Now, shall I take you home?"

"There's one more favor I have to ask," I said, glancing out the window at the darkening sky. "Can we go by Edith's and speak to her daughter, Lola? I'm worried about what she's up to in Edith's house."

Pua gave me a long stare, then shook her head. "No. You clearly need rest. You might have forgotten the post office, but I haven't. That's your primary job. I'm taking you home so you can be ready for work tomorrow."

I had no gas left in my personal tank to argue with her because Pua was right. I had to show up and open the post office tomorrow. Sharkey wouldn't be ready to drive, but hopefully I could get a ride or take my e-bike over to Edith's after work and check on that situation myself.

Whatever Lola was doing at Edith's house would have to be ignored for another day.

I leaned my seat back, closed my eyes, and let my frenemy drive me home.

29

"KAT. WE'RE AT YOUR PLACE." A voice in my ear, a hand on my arm. I started awake and flung my elbow up, cracking the perp in the head.

"Ow!" Pua recoiled, covering her cheek with her hands.

"Oh, slug manure! I'm so sorry. I'm dangerous to be close to when I wake up." The memory of Mr. K on the floor of my shack, paper towels stanching the blood streaming from his nose after he tried to wake me with a kiss, flashed into my mind. "Are you okay?"

Pua lowered her hands. Her cheek was red and already swelling. "Maybe some ice."

"Of course." The sensor light at my shack was on, though it wasn't yet full dark. I opened the Honda's door and got out.

My familiar attack cat was seated on the beach rock that made my top step, her kinked tail switching. The hibiscus and ginger plants were blooming. The baby palm tree in the rain gutter fluttered its leaves at me. My little shack looked and felt like home after a busy, stressful weekend.

"Hello, Tiki. Sorry I've been gone two nights and it's so late on a Sunday when I finally roll in. Will you forgive me?" I expected the stray cat's usual hissing, resentful greeting—but this time Tiki padded toward me, her tail up and swaying from side to side, her ear pricked.

I stood stock-still in astonishment as she wound her big body gently around my legs, purring like an engine with a bad mix in the carburetor. Her coat felt like a feather boa caressing my shins, infinitely rare and precious. I didn't want to break the spell, so I stood holding my breath and enjoying Tiki's affection with my eyes closed until Pua coughed delicately from the car. "I'd appreciate that ice, please. My face is swelling."

Tiki noticed we weren't alone. She leapt "like a scalded cat" (now I understood that phrase) away from my side and onto the porch, where she stood in front of the door. She yowled loudly in a tone of outrage and glared in my direction. This was much more like our usual communication pattern.

I did a quick assessment: the water dispenser I'd bought and left on the porch was still plenty full, but the metal food bowl Opal had monitored in my absence was empty. I hurried to the porch, fumbling in my backpack for the keys and undoing various locks I'd had to add to the door ever since bodies started happening in our little corner of paradise.

"Come on in, pretty girl," I said, opening the door and pulling the string that activated the overhead bulb. Tiki trotted inside. "I'll get your food."

Miss Prissy the cane spider and Tweedledum and Tweedledee, the resident geckos, were clustered above the stove in anticipation of the evening's bug feast. "Hey, guys." I stepped indoors, hung my backpack on its hook, and hurried to fill Tiki's bowl in front of the sink with kibble.

I then fetched the old-fashioned aluminum ice tray from the tiny fridge's freezer. I dumped a handful of ice cubes into a couple of paper towels and put the tray back in for later in case I needed some.

I headed back out to the car, going around to the driver's side.

Pua rolled down her window and I handed her the makeshift ice pack. "Here you go. I'm sorry for . . ."

"No need to explain." Pua flapped a hand dismissively as she took the ice. "I've seen your reflexes in action." She had, the day I flipped her nephew onto his back when he over-hugged me. "I should have known better than to touch you when you didn't see it coming."

I opened the back door and reached in for my bag of groceries. "Sorry anyway. One of these days I hope to be better. Meanwhile, thanks so much for everything—picking me up, the urgent care, the call to Terence." I straightened, my arms around the bag. I met her gaze. "I hope we can be friends, Pua."

Pua inclined her head and smiled as she held the ice to her cheek. "Hazardous as it is, I'd like that too."

"Kat? Pua? Is that you?" Opal's loud voice cut through our budding friendship gaze-fest.

I peered over the top of the Honda at Opal. The light from the general store's porch lit up her halo of spiky white hair. Her scarf of the day was electric blue, and a rhinestone pin caught the light and dazzled me all the way from across the parking lot. "I'm back, Opal! Thanks so much for feeding Tiki."

"Hi Opal." Pua got out of the car, still holding the makeshift ice pack to her face. "Do you have a minute to talk?"

I hoped Opal did. The women had been close friends before Pua's arrest. Opal told me how betrayed she felt by Pua's skullduggery—not so much that Pua ran drugs through the post office, but that she hadn't told Opal about it.

"Come over and have a sit on the porch, Pua. You too, Kat. I want to hear what's been going on. I'll get us something to drink and a snack." Opal disappeared back inside the store.

"Opal's been missing you," I told Pua. "But she was blindsided by your arrest. I hope you two can patch things up. I'll leave as soon as I can and give you space to talk privately."

"Thanks," Pua said. "She wasn't taking my calls, so I knew she was upset."

"Give me a minute to put my groceries away, and I'll be right over."

Pua nodded and set off.

Stiffness from the accident was setting in as I walked toward the store a few minutes later. I pictured the Murphy bed strapped to the wall of the shack with longing. My own little nest waited for me, with my cat to welcome me home—and a Tylenol PM or two to ease my way into dreamland. But if I could help Pua and Opal break the ice, I owed it to both women to try—so I put one size eleven in front of the other, all the way to the porch of the general store.

30

"HERE YA GO." Opal handed Pua a canned passionfruit-orange-guava juice (known in Hawaii as POG) and me an artisanal small batch Maine root beer in a squat brown glass bottle. "I ordered some of these special for you, Kat. Let me know if you like it."

"Omigosh, Opal. This brand takes me right home to the backwoods of my home state. Thanks so much." I cracked the top with the battered metal beer opener tied to a string on the railing. Pua and Opal settled in the two wooden armchairs the Pahinuis used most mornings to greet the day, so I unfolded one of the canvas seats they kept on hand for visitors. Opal opened a canned white wine and took a sip. "What's going on with you two? You look beat up. Did you get in a scrap? Beef with each other?"

"Scrap? Beef?" I took a swig of spicy, refreshing root beer. "I'm guessing that means a fight. The answer is yes and no."

"Kat got into an accident in the new car she was issued from her side job, and I picked her up on the shoulder of the road. I took her to the urgent care. On the way home, she fell asleep. I woke her up and got an elbow to the head," Pua explained. She lowered the wad of sodden paper towels and ice to grimace at Opal. "You don't want to wake Kat up, ever."

"Sounds like it's been a rough day for both of you. That ice pack sucks. Let me get you a real one." Opal rose and hurried into the store.

Pua and I looked at each other, and then out at the view. "Opal fusses when she cares," I said. "This is a good sign."

A string of cars went by nose to tail, their lights cutting through the indigo velvet of evening in Ohia. The moon, almost full, rose over the ocean. Mynah birds chattered from a palm tree near the bay's cement pier.

Pua shut her eyes. Her face was pale and tired, the mark on her cheekbone a puffy bright red. "I can't stay long. Sassy is home alone and needs me."

Once upon a time, not long ago, Pua had been employed at the post office in a pivotal role, caring for her disabled nephew as well as her yappy little white dog. Her nephew was now locked up on murder charges, Pua had been fired, and she was facing a trial. Going home to her isolated little farm at the back of a valley outside of Ohia with only Sassy to greet her must be a lonely and depressing experience.

Opal returned, carrying an old-fashioned blue fabric ice bag, the kind my Aunt Fae used on my bumps and scrapes when I was growing up. "Here." She thrust it at Pua. "Put that on your face."

Pua took the pack and gingerly applied it.

I took the melting wad of paper towels from Pua and pressed it to my forehead to dull the throb where my airbag had slammed my face. "Pua told you what happened in a nutshell. Any questions?"

"Heck yes." Opal plopped into her chair, and it creaked in protest. "First of all, what's going on with Edith's health?"

I took a fortifying swig of root beer and filled her in, only censoring where Edith had been moved to after her discharge. "Sophie at Security Solutions offered me a job as a consultant. I thought it was a good opportunity to get some wheels and get paid for what I was already doing." I sighed. "Turns out I was wrong about that, but hopefully Sharkey isn't in the shop for too long."

"Sharkey?" Pua and Opal said at the same time.

"My nickname for the nice white SUV Security Solutions issued me." I set my empty bottle in the nearby recycling bin. "I've got to open the post office tomorrow morning, and I'm beat. Opal, do you mind if I leave Pua to fill you in on the rest?"

"Okay," both women said and glanced at each other.

I suppressed a smile as I folded the camp chair and set it with the others. "See you tomorrow."

I unkinked myself with a stretch and as I did, a pair of headlights turned into the parking lot and pulled to a stop in front of my shack. Someone was here to see me at an inconvenient time. Even in the dim light I recognized the dark green of Keone's Toyota Tacoma truck with surf racks.

I hurried down the steps of the store and sped across the sandy dirt and mud puddle parking lot toward the shack. I hadn't known I had any energy left, but wow—here it was, a draft of excitement/happiness that "gave wings to my feet." I now understood that old cliche, too.

Mr. K slammed the truck's door and moved toward me with equal vigor. "Are you okay?" His voice was taut with worry, his beautiful brown eyes wide.

I reached him and opened my arms. "Hug please. But gentle on my chest, the seatbelt bruised my ribs."

He embraced me gingerly, and tightened his grip when I returned the hug with enthusiasm. Next thing I knew we were kissing, and it was . . . *brain offline, everything else lit up*.

Clapping from the porch of the general store interrupted our romantic interlude.

"Get a room!" Opal hollered, and she and Pua cackled.

I was glad they were getting along again but didn't appreciate being fodder for their crone bonding. "Come inside. I have beer."

"You know how to get a guy, babe," Mr. K said with a grin. "That's the perfect line."

I smiled as I opened the door of the shack. Tiki shot out like a cannonball, taking a swipe at Keone's legs as she did so. He yelped and jumped back, but Tiki was already gone, vanished into the bushes. "Glad I'm wearing jeans this time. Last time she did that, your hellcat drew blood."

"Tiki's jealous. She's been alone the last two days," I said as I led him inside.

"Mama has three cats and none of them act like that," Keone grumbled, taking a seat at my little table.

"Tiki's special." I reached inside the little fridge and pulled out a bottle of root beer. "Here ya go."

He took it, looked at me, and laughed. "I thought you said beer!"

"That is beer," I smirked.

He patted his lap. "Come here and tell me about your day. That message you left gave me gray hairs. I need to hear all the details."

I eyed him. "I'm stinky from a car crash and a walk toward Hana on foot."

"I don't mind." He patted his lap again. "And I wouldn't mind picking up where we were when we were interrupted by the aunties, either."

"Well, I mind. But you can warm up the bed while I take a shower."

His pretty eyes sparkled. "If you're proposing I spend the night, the answer's yes. I even brought my shave kit and uniform for tomorrow cuz I was hoping you'd ask me."

My face went warm as I remembered our last overnighter and how I'd got a bit closer to losing my virginity. I had been happy about that, but right now seemed too much too soon. "I think we need to go back to platonic tonight. I'm pretty tired and achy and I need to get up early for work tomorrow."

If he was disappointed, Mr. K hid it well. "You're driving this relationship bus and I'm okay with whatever speed it's going."

Something about that didn't sit right with me. I frowned and put my hands on my hips. "Banana."

"Oh, the safe word. We haven't used that in a while." We had come up with "banana" for when we needed to pause and talk about something in our relationship. He sipped his root beer. "What did I say?"

I pulled out the second chair and sat, gathering my thoughts. "Maybe I don't want to be in charge of the 'relationship bus' as you called it. I've been trying, Keone. I remembered to call you and leave a message about what happened this weekend. I'm glad you're here. I want . . ." I covered my face with my hands, embarrassed. "A lot of things. But I'm feeling weird about . . . us."

He gently tugged my hand until I lowered it, gazing into my eyes. "Weird—how?"

"I was so happy to see you . . . that it made me scared." I shut my eyes, overwhelmed. "I need that shower."

I tried to get up, but Mr. K was still holding my hand. He gave a little tug, and suddenly I was sitting on his lap. "I need you to be close to me while we talk about this," he said.

"Okay. I guess." I leaned away, rigid, my touchphobia activated. I perched on his knees like a crane on a tree branch.

"Kat, I was so glad when I got your message. Yes, I was freaked out that you were in an accident, that you've accepted a dangerous job, and that you can't seem to stay away from murder. But your courage is one of the things I like most about you. So, you're not the only one who's a little confused and scared about . . . us."

I still couldn't look at him, but I relaxed a bit and leaned against his chest. I watched Tweedledee (or was it Tweedledum?) zoom over and grab a moth; its wings stuck out from the gecko's mouth like a fan, and then gradually disappeared.

"Thanks for telling me that," I said at last.

"When I saw you coming toward me from the general store, that confused/scared thing got bigger as I saw your face and the way you were moving. You were in pain. But I was so glad to see you at the same time, that it all disappeared when you reached me . . ."

I turned and kissed him. That went on for a bit.

Finally, I drew back. "It seems like we're both a bit conflicted about . . . bananas."

He smiled and patted my butt. "Want some company in the shower?"

"Not tonight," I said.

"No worries." The way Keone held my gaze told me he meant it. "Take your time. I'll be here enjoying my delicious . . . beer."

This guy.

31

ANA:

The word MOM lit up the screen of my phone, right as I was changing the song I was listening to while I got a massage. I stared at the device in my hand a moment, battling the impulse to refuse the call—but I needed to know what she was up to on Maui. Mom could still mess things up for Fabio and me pretty easily.

I turned my head to the side and shut my eyes as I took the call through my earbuds. "Hey, Mom."

"I miss you. When are you coming over?" Mom sounded clearer than usual—strange for an evening call. She was usually three sheets to the wind by five p.m.

"Not sure," I hedged. We had no plans to go to Maui. "What's happening at Edith's?"

"Nothing. She's still recovering from the heart thing, from what I can tell. I'm bored. I need something to do. I can help."

She was already a hazard squatting in Edith's house, but Fabio was right. She was drawing the attention of Edith's protectors and the cops while our assassin worked in the background to take out our targets. "You could get a map. Plot likely places she could be moved to once she gets out of the hospital. Find out where her friends live. That could help us." The masseur dug his thumbs particularly deep into the notches above my waist. I stifled a moan of pain/pleasure.

"I guess I could do that. The general store in Hana has a detailed map." She sounded energized. "I have to return the rental car to the extension office. I only had it for a couple of days, but it's not far and I need to go there anyway. I'm running low on food."

And booze. That would explain her unexpected sobriety. "Thanks, Mom. I know you want to help. I'll be in touch if anything important comes up. Bye." I ended the call, and this time I put the phone in airplane mode so I wouldn't be disturbed.

I deserved all the good times I had coming after dealing with Mom and her disease all my life. So far, Fabio was the best thing to happen to me in a long time. Maybe ever.

I turned my head the other way to look at him, lying on a massage table beside mine. His masseuse was female, and she was working on his excellent glutes, an enjoyable sight. These couples massages were fun.

Fabio's dark eyes were open, watching me, and I liked that, too. "You okay?"

"Had to give Mom something to do to keep her busy. Can't have her getting up in our business."

He smiled. "You've got that right. Everything's going to be fine as soon as our guy gets his job done."

I shut my eyes and savored that thought as the masseur applied some muscle to my tight shoulders. I could get used to this life. In fact, I was born to live this way.

32

THE NEXT DAY, the rhythm of the post office's demanding but routine, non-complex tasks drove thoughts of the investigation out of my mind, and that was a relief for eight or so hours—though I had to revisit the story of being run off the road every time a customer asked about my puffy face.

Mrs. Vehikite, a short middle-aged woman who worked in Hana as the school nurse, was so bothered by my story and appearance that she came back after picking up her mail to give me a chilled, ripe native Hawaiian noni fruit in a Ziploc bag. "I've been saving this in case I needed it for a student or something, but I think you need it more." She handed the translucent, yellowish, cold knob of fruit to me. "Noni smells terrible but smoosh it up and put it on your face tonight before bed. You'll be amazed at how the swelling goes down in the morning."

Josie had educated me on the many health benefits of noni, but it looked like an alien had laid an egg and smelled like roadkill, so I'd been squeamish to use it. Even so, I couldn't refuse such a thoughtful gesture from a nurse, who presumably knew what she was talking about. "Thanks," I said. "I'll try it."

Mrs. Vehikite pulled out a pair of brown gradient aviators from her purse. "Someone forgot these at the school, and I thought you could wear them until your face is better."

I slid the glasses on gratefully. "I'm not supposed to accept valuable gifts, so I'll consider this a loan and put them back in your box at the end of the day. You're an angel."

"Please, no. They're knockoffs and not valuable. I was taking them to the lost and found. Wear them until you look better, and you won't have to keep showing everyone what an airbag to the face looks like."

"That would be a relief," I agreed and thanked her again.

What wasn't a relief was the just before closing visit of the Nakasone girls. I was learning to tell them apart. Sandy, the older one, was a hair taller than Windy, but otherwise indistinguishable. As often happened, Sandy carried the key and got to the box first while Windy lingered in the lobby to harass me.

"I warned you." The little hooligan sashayed over, swinging her hips. "You need to stay away from Keone Kaihale. I'm marrying him when I get older. He's mine."

I blinked at the scruffy-haired girl in front of me. She could barely see over the counter to give me the stink eye. "How old are you?"

"Old enough to know what I want."

I had a distinct sense of deja vu. "We've had this conversation before, haven't we?"

"That's why I shouldn't have to tell you twice."

Sandy relocked the box and approached, the lollipops I kept stashing in their box to sweeten the girls' tempers tucked out of sight among the junk mail. "No make *pilikia*, Windy. He's out of your league."

"And out of hers, too!" Windy yelled. She turned to me. "Go home to the mainland, *haole*! This is our town, and we want Auntie Pua back!"

The passion and anger behind the girl's words hit me like blows, and I was already bruised. I was glad I was wearing the sunglasses Mrs. Vehikite had given me because my eyes filled. I'd never spent much time around kids and didn't know how to talk to them, but these girls seemed way older than their ages. I was at a loss, so I said nothing, my stoic mask in place.

Sandy grabbed Windy's arm and dragged her sister toward the exit. "Sorry, miss," she said over her shoulder. "Windy has low blood sugar and gets grouchy when she's hungry."

The minute they were outside the door, she let go of Windy's arm. I watched through the glass as Sandy unearthed the two lollipops I'd put in the box from among the letters. She held out one to her sister.

Windy stared at it then said something (no doubt nasty) to Sandy. She slapped the candy out of her sister's hand and stomped off across the parking lot.

Sandy glanced back at me, shrugged, and leaned over to pick up the pop. She dusted it off, unwrapped it, and put the candy in her mouth, following her sister.

Well, my bribe had worked on one of the girls, but I was seriously concerned about the other. No little girl should go hungry, no matter how rude her behavior.

Ignoring my next customer, I went to the directory of boxes, looked up Mrs. Vehikite's contact info, and copied down her number. She lived a block away on Plumeria Street. I'd call her and see if there was anything more that could be done for the Nakasones.

The last rush of general delivery mail pickups went by, and I closed up the post office. I was tired but also revved to take my bike out, check on Edith's house, and see what Lola was up to. But first I had that phone call to make.

I rang Mrs. Vehikite. When she answered, I thanked her again for the glasses and the noni and then said, "I'm worried about the Nakasone girls. Do you see them at school?"

"They're absent more than I'd like."

I cleared my throat. "Sandy said something about being hungry. Is there a food bank or anything available to them?"

"Not out here. But I know some families who give them clothes and such. I'll make a few calls."

"I'd like to donate something to make sure they have food. Would it be okay if I bought some groceries at the general store and dropped them by your house? I don't think they'd accept anything from me directly."

"Sure. I'll take whatever you bring by to them." Mrs. Vehikite sounded surprised.

"And while I have you on the phone—is the word 'haole' derogatory?"

A pause. "Um . . . it can be. It means 'without breath' in Hawaiian. When the Polynesians saw whites for the first time they were alarmed by their pasty complexions." She gave a little chuckle. "The tourists' legs can be scary, the first time they see the sun. Anyway, it's come to mean Caucasian person, and depending on the usage, it can be descriptive or derogatory." Mrs. Vehikite sighed again. "I hope you don't take it personally if you heard it used in a negative way. We're glad you're here in Ohia, Kat. You've done a lot for our town in a short time."

My eyes prickled again; I didn't usually get so darned emotional. "Thanks for saying that. I'll be by with those groceries in a bit." I ended the call, feeling conflicted. How long was I going to be here in Ohia? I'd declined one Secret Service reposting opportunity already. It was possible I'd never get another, or one could come next week.

When I told Opal that the groceries I filled a bag with were for the Nakasone girls, she insisted on adding more until the paper sack was nearly bursting. "I usually leave our day-old baked goods and produce and such in a box for them on the porch, but we've been selling everything lately, and it slipped my mind," she said. "We've got to get more organized in helping them."

Everyone in Ohia seemed to know about the family's situation and be committed to helping. "I can't take any more than this sack, Opal. I'm dropping this stuff off at Mrs. Vehikite's on Plumeria Street from my bike, and the carrier is small."

"Then I'll fill a box and take everything over myself after I close up the store," Opal insisted. "You go over to Edith's and get an eyeball on that no-good Lola for us." My friend put her hands on her hips. "How did it go last night? I notice Keone stayed over again." Today's pin, a gold-plated dragon with big fake ruby eyes, winked at me suggestively from a red velour scarf.

I slid the big sunglasses on to hide my blush. "It's . . . not like that."

Opal rolled her eyes heavenward. "I wasn't born yesterday."

"It was a lovely platonic evening," I insisted, giving my sore chest a rub as I remembered how well I'd slept in Keone's arms. "We're friends."

"With benefits, if my eyes don't deceive me."

"Opal, please." I made prayer hands. "I'm not good at romantic relationships. When you and the other ladies tease us, it's hard to handle. Very awkward."

Opal's pale eyes softened, and she smiled. "Okay. I hear you, Kat. It's so fun for us old-timers to see. Keone has been the most eligible bachelor on the market for years, and until now he's shown little interest in anyone from around here."

"Well, I'm not from around here." A stab of pain tightened my chest. I rubbed the spot over my heart reflexively. "And I won't be here long. We're keeping it casual."

Opal shook her head and rolled her lips between her teeth, clearly holding back whatever she wanted to say.

"Here's all the cash I have. Put it toward the groceries for the girls." I plunked two twenties down, spun on my Nike, and headed for the door and my bike. Maybe on the ride to Hana I'd be able to think about what was going on between me and Mr. K without my heart going "bananas" and racing a mile a minute.

I kept the battery on its charger, so I was pleased to see it at full capacity as I wheeled the e-bike out and mounted up, wearing the lurid yellow helmet and vest Mr. K insisted were part of borrowing his mother's two-wheeler. Soon, I was whizzing toward Hana, loving the sensation of the wind whipping my ponytail and the cool breeze on my hot face. Cars could see me from a mile away in The World's Ugliest Helmet and Vest. They made a wide berth around me as I took the bends and curves of the jungle-engulfed road at around fifteen miles per hour.

As I rode, I flashed back to last night. I didn't blame Windy Nakasone one bit for her strong feelings for Mr. K. That guy was one in a million. After my shower, he'd taken one too, and changed into his beat-up University of Hawaii sweats while I pulled on my sleep tee and a pair of shorts for decency.

Then we'd fixed hot chocolate on the little stove and walked across the deserted highway to the beach with our mugs. We sat in sand still warm from the day as the moon came up to dance on the sea, and the palm trees waved their fronds with a soothing sound like a water rolling over stones.

I told Keone in more detail about the events of the day. "And that brings us to now," I concluded.

"I have a full workday with several flights to and from Hana tomorrow," he said. "So I'll be leaving super early in the morning. But if you have time after work, we should get in the ocean at Koki Beach. You need to go surfing and wash off all the stress from the weekend."

I told him my plan to go check on Edith's house after the P.O. closed. He said he'd meet me there if he got back from his flight on time. "Who knows what you'll find out there? I don't want you to go alone. And bring your gun," he said.

I didn't need to be told. My weapon was currently in its shoulder holster, hidden under the Ugly Yellow Vest. Hopefully Mr. K'd be able to meet me at the attorney's house. With someone like Lola, a witness was good to have.

Either way, I was ready for anything. Or so I told myself.

33

EDITH'S HOUSE was looking raggedy around the edges. The neat lawn had gone feral. Clearly, Lola also didn't know what to do with trash in this area. The metal rubbish can was overflowing and encircled by flies, and several bags of liquor bottles leaned drunkenly against each other beside it.

Edith's lime-green electric vehicle was now draped in clothing apparently hung to dry in the carport. Her sweet calico Butter was napping on the roof among the caftans and towels. The rental car Lola had arrived in was gone. Did that mean she was, too? Unfortunately, the granny panties dangling from the car's mirror spoke of someone who was settling in.

I put down the bike's kickstand and surveyed the place, my hands on my hips. "Amazing how fast she let it go to seed." Anger burned my chest—my friend was in bed, recovering from a heart attack, and helpless to stop this poacher on her preserve.

As a single woman, I don't pretend to understand the power dynamics between a mother and a daughter she'd given up for adoption. But I didn't have to. My job was to protect Edith, and that's what I was good at.

I was supposed to meet Mr. K before I approached the house,

but he hadn't yet arrived and maybe he wouldn't make it at all. I didn't have time, or patience, to wait and see. I headed for the front porch, where Edith's beloved orchids had wilted in the last week. "She's not going to be happy when she sees her babies looking like this," I muttered. I stepped up onto the lanai and rapped smartly on the door.

There was a good possibility Lola was out, since her car was gone—so I was surprised to hear a slurred, "whaddaya want?"

I tried the handle, and the screen door was unlocked. I opened it, and the main door behind it. "Lola? It's Kat." I sweetened my tone. I could do that. I'd worked for politicians.

"Kat? Who?" I stepped into a living room that looked like a clutter bomb had gone off. Lola had been asleep in the recliner, and she flailed her arms as if trying to swim up out of it. The interior was dim, the TV murmuring in the corner. Newspapers and pizza boxes were scattered over every horizontal surface. A map was spread open on the coffee table and held down at the corners by Edith's tchotchkes.

My curiosity antennae pricked at the sight of the map. I sidled closer to it while forcing a smile in the direction of the woman in the chair. "I thought I'd stop by and give you a report on how your mother is doing."

Lola pulled the recliner's lever. The apparatus tilted her upright. She used both hands to scoop unkempt blonde hair out of her face. "I was taking a nap. Who are you again?"

"Kat Smith. The postmaster. A friend of Edith's." I dropped the smile. "Love what you've done with the place."

Lola didn't appear to notice the sarcasm. She hauled herself out of the couch potato cradle with a grunt. She wore one of Edith's purple caftans, a favorite I'd seen my friend wearing with her red hat. The loose dress looked the same on Lola's barrel of a body as it did on Edith's. The anger tightening my chest dissolved; this was Edith's daughter. My friend loved this woman.

"I haven't been feeling well," Lola said. "How's my mother?"

"She's recovering. She'll be home soon." Subtlety was lost on Lola so far, so I walked over and stared at the map. It was a detailed schematic of the island and not one of those tourist things. A pencil rested on it and bottle caps were set here and there as if marking possible locations.

I was looking at some kind of plan to find Edith.

The hairs on my arms stood up. My hand slid over to touch my weapon in its holster. Anger was back, in spades. I was in no mood to deal gently with Lola now that I was pretty sure she, or an associate with her help, was using that map to look for Edith with murder on their minds. Plus, Lola was trashing my friend's house while up to no good. She was a sloppy drunk, and that was never attractive.

I narrowed my eyes at Lola. "Who else has been here?"

"What? Nobody." Lola scowled. She shuffled toward the kitchen, tugging Edith's purple caftan into place. "I know the cops are looking for Ana. I have no idea where my daughter is, so save your breath."

I glanced back at the map. Lola didn't have the wherewithal to hunt for Edith herself or be behind the black SUV that had run me off the road, but someone was behind that map on the table. Maybe that someone had taken her vehicle. "Where's your rental car?"

"I returned it." Lola clattered through the pile of dirty dishes in the sink, apparently looking for a clean glass.

If Lola had driven back to Kahului to return the car, how had she gotten all the way back here? On a plane? This was something I could check on easily. If there was no rental return in nearby Hana, I would conclude someone else had her rental car, because it was clear Lola wasn't up to driving that gnarly road to Kahului in her current state. The woman was in the middle of a bender.

Lola finally located a clean glass, filled it from the tap, and drank thirstily.

She didn't offer me anything, and I realized belatedly that the bike ride to Hana had dehydrated my body. One root beer with

Opal hadn't been enough as a *"pau hana"* beverage when followed by more physical exercise.

I followed Lola into the kitchen, wrinkling my nose at the smell of the trash bin. I found a clean mug in a cupboard and helped myself to a cup of tap water. "Thanks for the drink."

"Is my mother still in the hospital?" Lola turned to face me. The soft light of a Maui evening beamed through the window over the sink and illuminated deep, unhappy lines beside her mouth. Her bright blue eyes, the color of Edith's, were bloodshot. Pouches of unhealthy-looking flesh hung beneath them.

I almost felt sorry for her. Almost.

"No. Edith's been discharged. Like I said, she's recovering well. She's staying with a friend. But she'll be back soon. I suggest you pick things up a bit." I made a vague gesture encompassing . . . everything.

"Listen. There's something I need to tell you." Lola blinked rapidly. Were those tears I glimpsed in her eyes?

She was having a guilt attack. I was about to get some important information. I hopped on the moment like a mynah on a mango. "Whatever it is, you can tell me. I'm a friend," I cooed. I was a friend all right . . . of Edith's!

The roar of Mr. K's truck engine came through the open window as my maybe-boyfriend rolled up the driveway in his green Tacoma. Lola snapped her mouth shut and turned to face this new threat. Dangnabbit! The moment was lost.

I touched Lola's arm gently with a fingertip to get her attention. "That's my friend here to give me a ride—I came over on my bike. What were you going to tell me?" I asked softly.

"Nothing." When Lola turned back to face me, her gaze was empty as the bottom of a black bucket. "You've seen what you came to see. Now get out."

Anger was back, this time a roaring fire that swept up my body from my toes and made every muscle vibrate with the need to throttle something. "Edith changed her will, you know."

"What?" Lola deflated like a popped balloon and clutched the edge of the sink for support.

"Yep. Edith thought better of giving you a reason to hope she passed on. She got her lawyer in to do it up official and everything." Pure lies. But I didn't just want to hit Lola where it hurt—I wanted to see what this news flushed out.

34

Mr. K pounded on the door of Edith's cottage. I could tell by the urgency in the knock that he was worried for me. The original idea of having him join me here had gone all wrong, and it was destroying my chance to get a guilt-induced info dump out of Lola.

Now I had to deal with a guy's protective instincts on top of trying to get Lola to talk. Irritation flushed my body with prickles that made me twitch with annoyance. "Just a minute!" I hollered toward the door.

Lola clung to the edge of the sink, clearly in shock at the news about the will. (Good! Now I needed to convince Edith to follow through on cutting her out.) I had no patience for any of it, truth be told. I wanted to know who was after Edith and me!

Keone pounded again.

"Hold that thought. You were going to tell me something important," I told Lola. "Like I said, that's my friend." I turned toward the front door. "We're fine, Keone!" I bellowed in my Secret Service crowd control voice as he thumped on the door again. "I'll meet you at the truck!" The pounding at the door stopped. I could see Mr. K in my mind's eye, standing there, frowning, and trying to decide what to do.

Lola rallied. Anger was energizing her, too. "Oh heck no, Kat the postmaster or whoever you are. You and your 'friend' can both get lost," Lola snapped. "I'm sick and tired of Edith's people dropping by multiple times a day."

Just then, Keone opened the door.

Of course he did. He wanted to make sure Lola wasn't holding a gun to my head or something, not that this sad sack could ever have gotten the drop on me. Standing in his shoes, I would have opened up to check, too.

Lola snapped at the sight of him. "Get OUT!" She screeched, and hurled the glass she was holding across the room, toward the front door.

Keone ducked back outside.

The glass shattered against the screen backed by the wooden front panel. Glass flew everywhere. Lola reached for another dish, this time a china plate, and cocked her arm, aiming at me. "GET OUT!"

I raised my hands in surrender. Clearly our conversation was over. I didn't want Edith to lose any more dishes. "All right, all right, I'm going." I hurried through the living room, feeling Lola's furious gaze on my back. I crunched through the glass and opened the door. "You better clean this up," I said over my shoulder. "This is not your house."

Lola let out a howl like a wounded animal and hurled the plate. I barely got the door shut behind me when the thing broke against the wood with a sound like a grenade going off.

"Wow, Kat, you really canned her pineapple," Keone said from the front yard below the porch.

I cringed at the sound of more bellows of anger and plates crashing into furniture. "I did a bad thing in there. I told Lola something she didn't want to hear . . . and it wasn't true. I wanted to get her to tell me who was behind the attacks. But now Lola's breaking all Edith's dinnerware."

Even in the midst of the storm inside the house, I couldn't help but notice that Keone was still wearing his clingy white polyester uniform trimmed in gold braid. I loved the way he looked in it, a cross between disco-ready John Travolta from Saturday Night Fever and a fantasy stripper dude in a pilot costume.

But now wasn't the time to comment on that. "Should we call the cops?" I wondered aloud.

"You're the one in law enforcement. What do you think?"

A resounding crash, followed by another howl, goosed me into action. "Yes. They can kick her out of the place now. There's justification." Then I paused, holding my phone. "But wait. I want to see who Lola calls to talk about the will. Maybe it will be Ana."

"What did you tell her about Edith's will?"

"Later. Get your truck out of visual range. I'll move my bike, too, and then I'll have to sneak back here to use this surveillance device Sophie gave me to intercept her call." I patted the saddlebag on the bike. "Let's move."

Keone got into the truck and fired it up. He backed down the driveway.

I mounted my bike. Still angry at Lola, I turned to yell at the house. "You've shown your true colors, Lola. You never cared about Edith! You're trashing her stuff now that you're not inheriting it." I drew a breath. "Actions speak louder than words!" I have a voice, and I can project it pretty well.

The mayhem inside stopped for several seconds—then, another howl of rage split the air, but no further crashes accompanied it. I hopped on the bike, pleased that I'd goaded Lola into stopping her destruction. Hopefully, she'd pull herself together and call whoever she was working with (probably Ana) and share the bad news about her lost inheritance. I would intercept that call, record it, and notify the cops to have Lola removed from the premises.

But as I knew from field work, things often don't go according to best laid plans, and this plan wasn't developed at all—I was making it up on the fly. The potential for disaster was high.

I pedaled down the driveway to where Keone had parked his

truck on the main road. He jogged to meet me where I stashed the bike behind a clump of waist-high ferns.

I looked him up and down. "That white uniform is going to stand out. We need to get close enough to the house for me to use the spy device Sophie loaned me. You should wait in your truck."

Mr. K didn't miss a beat. He unbuttoned his shirt and ripped it off. Unzipped his pants and dropped them. Toed out of his shiny work shoes and socks. Stuffed the clothing into the ferns.

He straightened up before me. Brown muscles gleamed above a pair of camo print boxers that should have been visible through his white pants, but by some voodoo magic, hadn't been. "I blend with the forest now."

I gulped. "Yes. Yes, you do." I cleared my throat. "Okay. Let's do this." I fumbled in the bike's saddlebag and took out a black device that looked like something one of the Jetsons would have used as a weapon in the cartoon show. "This is called a Crossbow. It's very expensive."

"Cool. Can I see that?" Keone had a little-boy fascinated gleam in his eye as he reached for the pistol grip of the device.

I yanked it away. "No. Stay behind me and keep quiet."

I half expected Keone to get offended and take off in a huff, but I didn't have time to coddle his male ego. I set off at a jog down the driveway surrounded by jungle, back toward Edith's house. I'd already picked my target location for the phone call intercept—a decrepit old garden shed at the edge of the yard. I had to run across open space to get there, and I wanted to make sure Lola didn't see us. I watched and listened, crouched behind a tree across from the shed.

Keone caught up and stood unnecessarily close behind me. I could feel his breath on the back of my neck. I wished I hadn't seen what he was wearing; it was distracting.

I heard nothing from the house. Evening was still light enough for us to be easily visible should Lola look outside when we made our move, but I doubted she would be doing anything but refilling the highball glass I'd seen beside the recliner. She'd be picking her way through the rubble to sit on her borrowed throne and drown her sorrows while she made that phone call.

Or so I hoped.

35

INSTEAD OF CALLING RIGHT AWAY, though, Lola swept up glass. The sounds of broken dishes rolling around raised the hairs on my neck. I signaled to Keone and darted over to the shed. We hunkered down, getting comfortable, as the cleanup went on for fifteen minutes or so.

Finally, silence fell, and I turned on the Crossbow and put in its accompanying earbuds. I adjusted the sound on the earbuds and pointed it at the window of the living room to intercept Lola's call. I hit the "Record" button and watched a readout screen on the top of the device that tracked the strength of the signal. The wavy lines looked okay, and I could make out Lola's words, but what did I know about what was going on?

I'd never used the thing before. I'd read the specs on it during my lunch break at the P.O. and knew how to activate, intercept, and listen to a call, and record the call on the chip inside the device for later download and analysis. Or at least theoretically. The stakes were high for a first-time use on a fancy piece of technology with no rehearsal.

"Hey, Mom." A young female voice. This must be Ana. My pulse picked up. "Did you get the map like I told you?"

"There'sh been a change of plan, Ana." Lola's words were slurred—yep, she'd slammed another drink or three between when I surprised her awake in her recliner, her dish-throwing fit, the cleanup, and this phone call. "Edith changed her will. I'm out."

"I'm betting that huge woman Edith's got guarding her is behind this," Ana said.

My hackles rose. I'd never met Edith's rogue granddaughter, but I objected to being called "huge." I was six foot one inch tall, it's true. But otherwise, my proportions were normal. "Meanie," I muttered under my breath.

"What?" Keone's whisper lifted hairs on my neck that were exposed by my ponytail. I'd forgotten he was there. "What's going on?"

"I've picked up the connection," I whispered back. I didn't turn my head to look at him because I didn't want to see him in his skivvies when I was trying to focus and be professional. I held the Crossbow up so he could watch the wavy lines instead. Hopefully that would keep him busy while I listened in.

"She's come by here twice," Lola slurred. "Kat's trying to get rid of me."

"Yeah? Well, we've decided to get rid of her. Sit tight, Mom."

Confirmation that Ana and the Changs had extended their hit to include me hollowed my stomach. My belly growled unhappily.

Lola's sigh was long. I could almost smell the alcohol fumes on her breath. "I made a mess here. I don't want to stay anymore. I think I'll go to the Hotel Hana."

"Mom! You don't have any money. That's why you had to take that rental car back." Ana's voice went sharp with irritation. "Clean the place up and sit tight. I'll look into the will thing more closely. I have eyes on Edith from another direction and according to my intel, she's barely functional. No sign of a lawyer, at least while she was in the hospital."

Lola's voice perked up. "So maybe she didn't change her will?"

"Let me check into it, at least." A beat went by. "I'll come soon.

Stay put. And clean up that house. I won't set foot in it until you do."

A buzz of static and an end to the wavy lines told me the communication was over. I switched off the recording feature, but kept the device aimed at the house in case Lola made another call. Maybe she had a Chang to notify or something.

Several minutes went by. I became aware that I was leaning against the old shed's splintery wall and a mosquito or seven had discovered my extremities. Mr. K was standing way too close for comfort.

"Just waiting a bit more to see if she reaches out to anyone else," I whispered.

"Okay."

The mosquitoes zinged around my head with their high-pitched yodeling. I could hear them even through the earbuds.

"Okay. She's done." I switched off the Crossbow and stuck it in my waistband, then popped out the earbuds and slipped them into their case. I turned around and collided with Mr. K. "Dude. What are you doing?"

"Watching you," he said, sparkling his eyes at me. "You're so hot when you're investigating."

"Ugh. Stop it. We're on the job and this is serious." I brushed by his mostly naked body and trotted across the open space into the tree line. I paused there to see if Lola had noticed us—not a ripple from the closed curtains in the windows.

Mr. K stuck to me like Velcro. I frowned at him. "How are you not attracting mosquitoes with all that . . ." I gestured . . . uncovered skin?"

"They like tender white flesh from tourists straight off the plane. I don't even get bumps anymore." Keone held out a bronzed, muscled arm to show me where a mosquito had landed and was doing its best to drill for blood to no avail. "See? Don't even react to them."

I saw all right. "I'm out of here." I used my post-mission adrenaline to run down the driveway and flee the little monsters. Keone was right behind me.

We reached the stand of ferns. I removed the bike while Mr. K found his uniform. "There's still enough light for an evening surf session at Koki Beach," he told me. "Let's throw your ride in the back of my truck and go."

I was itching from head to toe with mosquito bites; the critters had bit me through my clothing. The thought of cool water soothing my skin was appealing. "Perfect. But I need to call Lei and Sophie. Also, food too. You know how I get when I'm hangry."

"Got it covered. I picked up a couple of meals to go in Kahului before my last flight back to Hana. Went to a restaurant you'll like, so you have that to look forward to after we get out of the water."

"Sounds perfect." And it did.

SUNSET STREAKED the water at Koki Beach with orange and salmon pink as Keone and I surfed small waves that rolled in over the sand bottom.

Or, he surfed.

I floundered, wallowed, paddled madly, wiped out, churned my arms, and otherwise flopped around—a total "kook" as lame surfers were called around here.

Still, it felt amazing to forget about the nasty dialogue I'd heard on the Crossbow and the follow-up calls to my law enforcement pals. I threw myself into attempting to master a sport that clearly took a lot of practice. As Keone whizzed by on his longboard, one foot extended to hang his toes off the nose while doing the dab with his arms, I laughed out loud. That felt good too.

I stood up from my latest wipeout in the shallow water near shore and rearranged my bikini back to decent. Keone glided up and stepped off his board into the shallows. He hadn't even gotten his hair wet the whole time. "Show-off."

"Just trying to impress my girl."

I scooped up a handful of water and threw it at him. "Now your hair is wet."

"Oh it's like that, is it?"

We splashed each other and tussled about. The last of the angst I felt over what I'd heard spying on Lola and Ana washed away in the sea foam and sunset. I grabbed the board he'd loaned me and dragged it clumsily up onto the sand. "I'm starving. Where's that food you promised?"

"Go rinse yourself and the board off and we'll eat in the hut."

I followed directions. I could do that on occasion, especially when food was promised. By the time I'd washed up, the temperature had dropped as the sun hid behind the mountains. Hana caught the sunrises, and Lahaina on the west side got the sunsets in the geography of this particular paradise island.

Keone wrapped a warm towel around my shoulders as I stowed the board on the racks over his truck bed. "Mm. How do you get your beach towels warm like that?"

"Can't give away all my secrets." He thrust his board up beside mine onto the truck's racks. "Let's eat."

The food was from a Vietnamese restaurant in Kahului. I shoveled in a delicious rice and pork dish and smacked my lips over seasoned beef on skewers, finally topping up my belly with a bowl of savory pho.

Keone eyed me admiringly as I slurped the last of my noodles. He was still on his skewers. "You know how to put it away, lady."

I patted my abdomen. "Yep. Takes a lot to fuel this machine." I cracked the top on the beer he'd handed me and took a sip.

I was glad he hadn't asked what I'd picked up on the Crossbow. I wasn't ready to tell him there was a hit out on me, too.

I tightened the towel around my body and walked over to the truck, retrieving my phone. Thankfully, Koki Beach was close enough to Hana to have some signal, and I thought over the calls I'd made when we first arrived.

I'd phoned Lei first, since she was tasked with locating Ana, and this was a lead. The sergeant detective picked up on her cell, and I filled her in rapidly about what I'd discovered at Edith's house.

"Anything you got that way is inadmissible in court," Lei said as I finished telling her the content of the intercepted call.

"Of course. I know that." I was indignant. "And I don't care. My priority is my client staying alive. That's officially my job now that I'm a Security Solutions operative on Edith's case. Cops have to worry about court testimony and chain of evidence. I don't envy you that." I frowned. "Anyway, speaking of cops—I called the Hana PD as Keone and I left, and hopefully they get Lola out of Edith's house since she trashed the place."

"I'm sorry, Kat. I didn't mean to sound rude about all the effort you went through to discover what Lola and Ana are up to. My brain was going a mile a minute thinking about all you've told me. I'm worried, is all. If the Changs have extended the contract hit to you as well, I don't know how to protect you."

"It's okay. That's what I'm good at," I said stoutly, but the wind off the sea had raised goose bumps all over me. "I'll be fine and so will Edith. Can you take care of calling Marcella about what happened? Because I need to update Sophie about how her Crossbow device came in handy. I want to hear how things are going with Edith from her, too."

"Sure." We said goodbye.

I made my next call to Sophie. She didn't pick up, so I left a long message. "Reach me at the post office tomorrow on the landline, Sophie, so we can talk. I want to know how Edith's doing. Hopefully the cops remove Lola from her house, and I can clean it up before she comes home, but with this news I don't think that should be anytime soon." I paused and pinched the bridge of my nose, feeling tired all of a sudden. "I'm responsible for setting Lola off with that lie about the will and I wish I hadn't done that, even though it got us more info."

I now stood up from the table and walked to the opening of the beach hut, wrapping my arms around the beach towel and myself for warmth. I gazed out over the darkening ocean, shivering. An 'iwa frigate bird flew by, a big black shadow against the indigo sky. The moon rose above the horizon, a gibbous yellow ball painting light over the restless sea.

Keone came up. "Okay for a hug?"

I nodded. He put his arms around me from behind. He rubbed big hands over my arms. "You've got chicken skin."

"You mean goose bumps."

"In Hawaii, they're chicken skin." His warm strength surrounding me felt . . . oh, so good. I relaxed, leaning into him. "I like how tall you are," he said in my ear. "I've never been the same height as someone I dated. I can put my chin on your shoulder." He did so, and it felt nice.

I turned in his arms so we were eye to eye. "Kissing is easy when you're the same height, too," I said. We tested that hypothesis.

"Ready to go home?" Keone rubbed my "chicken skin" arms.

"Please."

We walked back to the truck. Mr. K cranked up the heater as we got on the road toward Ohia. "I can't spend the night tonight," he said. "While you were on the phone, I got a notification too. I have an early flight tomorrow morning."

"It's okay." I wiggled my bare toes in the draft of hot air coming in under the dash. "I've got a few more calls I forgot. I'll have to open up the post office and use the landline. Then, it's straight to bed for me." I yawned so big my jaw cracked. "It's been a heck of a day."

Keone shook his head. "They all seem to be, lately."

I tightened the beach towel. "Isn't that the truth." A wave of apprehension brought a fresh crop of bumps to my skin as I thought about all the threats I needed to neutralize. "I can't wait for things to settle down around here."

36

Mr. K left for the night after a few more kisses. I didn't tell him about what Ana had said on the phone to Lola about getting rid of me. I'd handle this situation myself.

As I waved goodbye and Keone pulled away, I scanned the high ground of the bluff at the end of the bay. The village of Ohia's neat streets and small cottages rose behind my place, the post office and general store, toward the highest point of the town at the church up on the hill. Our little hub was at its lowest point.

And here I was, sniper bait, standing in the doorway of a decrepit shack whose construction had all the bullet stopping power of cardboard.

The smart play would be for me to go somewhere else, somewhere safe and hidden, until we'd dealt with the Chang threat, but I had a job to do at the post office. Of course, I could ask one of the Red Hat ladies or Keone to put me up for a bit—but where could I go that wouldn't draw danger to anyone who sheltered me?

I went inside the shack, my mind a million miles away, reached for the string to the lightbulb—and tripped over a large, furry object.

Tiki yowled and lashed out as I mashed her tail under my bare foot—a replay of our first meeting. I yelped and grabbed my bare, bleeding shin, hopping around on my good foot as the cat bolted into the bathroom. "Tiki, ow! I'm sorry, I was distracted!" Clutching my injured limb, I hobbled into the bathroom and turned on the light. "Tiki?"

The cat was gone.

The bathroom must be where her secret access to the shack was —Tiki had been appearing and disappearing in spite of the shack's locked door since I moved in. But this time I wanted to find her secret exit. It might be important.

I fetched my high-powered flashlight. I poked and prodded every board and corner in the bathroom. In the end, Tiki's "cat door" wasn't hard to find. Beside the corner shower stall, a deep, built-in shelf held towels, extra TP, and bathroom supplies. When I got on my knees and pressed against the wall under the shelf, the wood panel swung back to reveal the dark space of the post and pier foundation beneath the shack. I held the panel up and shone the flashlight around. The dirt under the shack looked disturbed. I'd found Tiki's litterbox. "Ew."

But the panel was big enough for me to crawl through, and the ground was only a couple of feet away. With a little wiggling I could fit through the opening and be outside in seconds.

Could I create a makeshift "safe room" under the house until I solved my dilemma about where to go?

The answer was yes, though my body began to ache and remind me it hadn't been long since I was in a car accident. I'd ignored that to ride a bike and go surfing. Now Body wanted Bed, but the night was still young. I had phone calls to make and a safe room to build.

I LOCKED up the post office and checked fore and aft for any signs of danger, after making my calls to the Red Hat ladies to update them.

No one was around but the bullfrog that lived in the jungle behind the shack, and he was ribbiting to beat the band. The village slumbered on the hill, lights out mostly. No disturbances but the shimmer and sigh of a gentle wind in the coconut palms.

I popped some ibuprofen and dressed in my worst set of old clothes, then put on a particle mask and rubber gloves. Cat poop is toxic, and I didn't want to get any on me. I lugged over a pile of folded cardboard boxes from deliveries at the post office that had been stacked behind the building for recycling. I had also procured a box cutter and some sturdy, clear plastic packing tape when I was over there.

I won't say the crude, roomlike fort I created under the shack was pretty, but it was functional. The sealed walls meant I could have a light on inside without being detected and keep mosquitoes out.

What I didn't count on was Tiki's annoyance that her kitty door had been appropriated. She appeared outside my cardboard shelter and meowed indignantly.

"I thought you were mad at me and left for the night, sweet girl." Like calling Tiki pretty, I hoped to influence her with the power of positivity. "Stay right there and I'll fix you a door."

I used the box cutter to carve a flap in one wall. I pushed it open and peeked through it at Tiki's face. My own special hellcat sat on her haunches looking puzzled, which meant her remaining ear was a little sideways and her whiskers were back. A bit of a crease in her tabby-colored forehead revealed confusion. Her eyes were wide open in the dim light, looking for answers to my bizarre behavior.

One of my training courses for the Secret Service had been "Reading Face and Body Cues," but none of it applied to Tiki. She was a feline, and yet I perceived her feelings and thoughts clearly and always had.

"Come on in, girl. I'm making a fort. It'll be fun. We can spend the night in here and go up into the house if we want. It's all good."

Tiki was not convinced. She licked her paw, glancing up at me suspiciously.

I moved the flap back and forth so she could see that it worked like the panel into the bathroom, and then I climbed out of my new "safe room."

Up in the house, I locked up. I showered and changed into my sleep tee, grabbed my sleeping bag, blow-up travel pillow, and e-reader, turned off the main lightbulb, and crawled into my cozy fort.

If someone shot up the shack with a machine gun, I'd be fine here.

If anyone came to the door with deadly intent, I could hide and assess the situation, watching them on my phone with the video surveillance node I'd installed over the door a while back.

I had two options to respond to a frontal assault on the shack's door: I'd left a couple of sheets of cardboard outside the fort so I could belly crawl to a spot near the beach rock step, where I could shoot an intruder in the leg. Or, if the numbers were too great and the firepower overwhelming, I could scuttle out the back into the jungle, which I knew well by now and could hide in with ease.

Tiki would be safe, too. She'd come with me; I was sure.

Yes, I felt safe in my cardboard shelter. That was a good feeling, even if the smell, musty and cat-poopy, wasn't so great. I left the flashlight on as I snuggled into the sleeping bag, and it made a circle of light that reflected off the cardboard wall, illuminating the space. The sleeping bag didn't provide a ton of padding, but enough to get by. I inflated the travel pillow, put it behind my head, and took out my e-reader. I switched my device on.

Soon, I was lost in a thriller, the story of an amazing mixed-race woman solving crimes in Hawaii using technology and some mad fighting skills. Wow, this lady had complicated relationships! Three men were in love with her and each of them was awesome. How could she choose, with killers to catch? I was glad to have ONE guy interested in me, though gosh knows why he was . . .

Tiki disturbed my reading trance by poking her head through the cardboard flap. "Are you joining me?"

She did, settling in a corner with a rumbling purr. The sound was so soothing that I switched off my device and flashlight and drifted off to sleep in a darkness so complete it felt like the womb.

37

TIKI BUTTED my head with her nose and made a sound like "merp." I woke up, blinking. The darkness inside the cardboard fort was absolute. "What is it, girl?" I whispered. Tiki butted me again—and this time, I heard a creak in the boards overhead, as if someone were standing on the porch near the front of the shack.

I gently moved one cardboard wall over and peered toward the porch area. No light showed, which was strange. The sensor bulb on the porch should have lit up when my visitor appeared.

I slid an arm over the cat and drew her close, fumbling to find my phone. I pressed the button on the side to check the time—two thirty a.m.

Not the hour for Keone to be stopping by. Besides, he wouldn't have been sneaking around, and that's what this person was doing. I thumbed to the phone app that surveilled the door, but when the video came on it was too dark to see anything. "Crud on a cracker," I whispered.

A high-pitched sound—PEW! (thock) PEW! (thock) PEW! (thock)—made Tiki jump. I bit my lips to keep from yelping aloud as the cat landed on my head and wrapped her body over it like a live fur hat with claws and teeth. I couldn't tell whether she was trying to hide behind or protect me, but I clamped both hands over the big cat's body, holding her still and in place, even though I was now breathing her armpit hair.

That sound we'd heard was the explosive spit of a silenced bullet slamming through wood.

A series of rapid creaks told me the assassin was leaving. Several breaths later, off in the distance, a vehicle roared into life.

If I'd been a betting woman, I'd have wagered that whoever tried to put three rounds in me while I was sleeping drove a big black SUV.

I lowered my hands and sucked in fresh oxygen as Tiki bolted out the opened side of the fort and disappeared. I rolled over and turned to crawl into the shack. As I stood up in the bathroom, I had to grab the sink as a wave of dizziness swept over me.

Someone had—totally, definitely, no ifs, ands, or buts—tried to kill me. This attempt was way more real and serious than the attempt at running me off the road had been.

My knees made like jelly as I flicked on the flashlight. I kept the beam low as I crept forward and verified that yes, the wall of my shack was pierced by three bullet holes and so was my pillow. A few bits of white feather spun lazily over the bed, caught in the bright flashlight beam.

Whoever did this was a pro. They'd cased the place at some earlier time because there was no window on the front side of the shack from which to aim at the bed. They had to have either seen inside when the door was open, or through the uncovered window at the back when I was gone.

"Okay, Kat. Time to call in the cavalry." My voice speaking aloud startled me. Sweat burst out of my pores. I began to shake. "You're in shock," I continued. "It's okay. You know what to do. Call for backup."

I was pretty certain the shooter acted alone and was gone, but it behooved me to be careful until I was sure. I longed to run sobbing to Opal and Artie's and be swept up in their love and concern, but I didn't want to bring trouble to the vulnerable couple's doorstep.

Instead, I would go inside the post office once I'd verified the coast was clear, barricade myself in, and call for help.

So that's what I did.

THE CRINKLY SILVER film emergency blanket was surprisingly warm, covering me completely, but I couldn't stop shivering. I'd been able to tell my story clearly without my teeth chattering to the first responders. Even so, relief swamped me when Lei, with Pono close behind, pushed past the two Hana cops who'd taken my statement as we sat inside the postal building.

"You're coming with us," Lei snapped. Her face was so serious that my eyes flew wide.

"I didn't do anything!" I exclaimed. "I'm the victim here!"

Pono clapped me on the shoulder. "Lei only barks at people she loves," he said, lifting me by an elbow.

"That's not true." Lei took my other elbow. "I'm known as 'Sweets' by a few special people, but it's not because I'm sweet."

The two detectives frog-marched me out of the post office toward a waiting van, both of them scanning for threats as we crossed the parking lot.

"We're taking you into protective custody," Pono explained as we approached the windowless black vehicle.

"How did you get here so fast?" I dug my heels in and stopped. "I can't leave the post office unlocked and not tell Opal and Artie what happened!"

"It's handled." Lei leaned into shoving me into the van, but I'm not easily moved, especially by someone so much smaller.

Pono rolled his eyes at our stalemate. "I'll go over and let Opal and Artie know what happened and where you're going. Meanwhile, the guys will lock up and call your boss at the post office for someone to fill in for you. Right?" He made eye contact with the two uniformed officers who'd responded to my 911 call.

"You got it, Detective Kaihale," one of them said. He took out his phone, holding it aloft for signal. There was none, so he headed across the street to the beach. The bars were better by the water and everyone appeared to know that.

"I'm off to wake up the Pahiniuis." Pono turned and strode off.

"This is probably overkill. The shooter did their thing and is done for the night, most likely," I said, tightening the crinkly blanket around myself and stepping up into the open van.

"Probably. Most likely," Lei echoed my words. "You said it, not me. And what about tomorrow when they find out you're still walking around?"

"Yeah, yeah." I folded myself inside the windowless van. It smelled of Lysol and vomit. "Tell me this isn't a prisoner transport vehicle."

"This was all we could get to drive you on such short notice."

"You never answered how you arrived so fast."

"Helicopter," Lei said. "Captain Omura authorized the flight when she heard you'd almost been shot. We'll take you to a safe house not far away."

My teeth chattered with the realization of how seriously everyone was taking this. "Th-that's nice. Okay."

"I have a feeling this case is coming to a head."

"Yep." I was mouth breathing a hundred percent due to the van's smell. "Things are escalating."

"We need the FBI to get something hard on whoever's behind New Ohia. Once we bring them down, the threat to you and Edith will go away," Lei said impatiently. She got into the passenger seat up front and put on her belt. "I've already called Marcella and told her we need her team to work faster."

"We also need to capture Ana," I reminded her. "Ana's the one driving the murder bus. And have you notified Sophie?"

"Yep. She's the one who arranged the safe house for you in

Hana. She says to tell you Edith is feeling better. She met with a lawyer to change her will."

"Oh, good. That's a relief." I flopped back against the plastic covered seat. "I don't think I told you. Pua Chang was the one to pick me up after the car accident. We called a relative of hers, Terence Chang, to tell him about what was going on. Supposedly he's the 'legit head of the family.' He said he'd look into it. Make some calls." I'd told Pua I'd keep this confidential, but I trusted Lei to handle it discreetly.

Lei smiled, an expression of evil glee. "Terence has come a long way since I first met him. We've worked together on several cases. We're friends—of a sort."

"He said he had his own contacts in law enforcement. You must be one of them." I was glad telling Lei hadn't backfired to hurt Pua.

I gazed out the open door of the van toward the shack. With the lights of the post office on, bullet holes were clearly visible in the wall, and so was a dangling LED bulb that had been loosened from my sensor light, probably during daylight hours.

"I'll have to call Opal and ask her to feed Tiki," I said.

"The cat will be fine." Lei smacked her hands on her jeans-clad thighs with an air of discharging energy. "Quit worrying about a feral animal."

"Tiki was the one who woke me up," I said. "She's very special."

"If you say so. I'm a dog person." Lei rubbed a white bone hook, clearly some kind of totem, between her thumb and fingers. Her eyes gleamed in the dim light. "Good news about Terence Chang, Kat. The most the FBI may be able to do is close New Ohia and appropriate the assets associated with it if they can't get enough evidence to connect the family to the development. But Terence can shut down any of his relatives who's getting out of line —permanently."

I tightened the crinkly blanket. My bare legs were getting cold. "That doesn't sound legit," I said.

"He's legit in the sense that he makes sure his hands don't get dirty."

"Ah." This discussion was creeping me out, and I wanted to get to bed. The aftermath of adrenaline overload had morphed into profound tiredness and still my body's tremors wouldn't stop. "I should go get some clothes and such since Pono is taking so long."

Of course, that's when Pono came jogging back, and he was carrying a plastic trash bag stuffed with clothing. My beloved Nikes were a visible shape from the side. "Thought you should have some basics since you might be gone a while. Opal said not to worry. She'll take care of your cat. She sends hugs."

"Oh good." I wrapped my arms around the bag as Pono handed it to me. I could feel toiletries as well as clothing inside. "I can tell this isn't your first rodeo."

"Nope, it's not. We've got your back, Kat." Pono slammed the side door and hopped into the driver's seat. Darkness fell inside the windowless, presumably bulletproof van. "Let's get you out of here."

It was weird for the protector to be the protectee. But as I slumped over on the bench seat and shut my eyes, curling around the plastic bag Pono had packed, I had to admit it felt pretty darn good to have these cops looking out for me.

38

THE PHONE BUZZING beside the bed in the safe house woke me. Disconnecting the power cord, I marveled at Pono's thoughtfulness in remembering to pack the charger. I swiped to answer the call from Sophie but didn't sit up. Instead, I stretched, sliding my limbs around in a shape like the snow angels I used to make in Maine in the winter, enjoying the smoothness of excellent sheets on a good mattress. "Hi, Sophie."

"How are you? Did you sleep all right?" My new boss's cool Brit voice was a tad pressured. In the background, I heard the high-pitched tones of young children in a squabble.

"Better than you." I scanned the wooden ceiling overhead, enjoying the natural handmade look of it. "This place is amazing."

"I'm glad you think so. The rental was billed as a tree house mansion. All I could find on such short notice, but it had the basics required for a safe house. I hope it's adequate."

"I'll say." I rolled over and gazed out through a sliding glass door that opened onto a little deck high above a view of the ocean. "This house built around a tree is crazy. I'm glad to have been shot at to get to stay here."

"Only you would say that Kat." I heard the smile in Sophie's voice. "I called to tell you that the FBI has formally seized all assets associated with New Ohia Vision, Inc. Today a tactical team will be arresting the project manager, Thompkins, and searching all buildings in the development for evidence."

"Finally!"

"Yes, it's been tough for the FBI to build a case. Then some of the buyers in the development realized they didn't actually own their properties there and launched their own complaint. They later recanted, but it was enough for a probable cause search. Marcella is hoping the raid will uncover something the FBI can use to tie in the Chang connection."

I sat up at last, tossing aside the silky bedding. I padded over to the slider and opened it, exiting to sit in an Adirondack chair on the lanai. The tropical air felt great wafting up from below the tree onto bare skin exposed by my sleep tee. From where I sat, the enormous banyan branches that supported the bedroom and deck swayed overhead and around me, creating the sensation of a gently rocking ocean liner. Dappled light moved through the leaves and fell over me like bright confetti. Below me, mowed lawn surrounding the tree house was clear and open with good visibility and sensor lights that came on with motion. Best of all, a tall fence topped with ornamental metal arrowheads provided a deterrent to unwanted visitors.

"Let's hope something breaks soon," I said. "The post office needs me."

"Not as much as the rest of us do," Sophie said. "Relax and recover. It's been a rough few days. I'll keep you updated." She ended the call after a particularly shrill bellow from one of her small humans.

I set aside the phone, leaned back my head, and closed my eyes, enjoying the gentle breeze and the green tinted sunlight on my face. I was safe here, and though there hadn't been time to post a Security Solutions operative with me, the Hana police were on speed dial and a couple of Maui detectives were asleep in the other rooms, at least for the moment.

I missed my cat, though.

That reminded me I missed Mr. K, too.

The bottom of my belly dropped away.

I hadn't called Keone about the attempt on my life or my relocation, and he'd specifically asked me to do that if anything big happened. Last night's shooting attempt qualified as something big.

But hopefully he hadn't been informed by the coconut wireless about recent events. I shoveled a handful of long, tangled brown bed head out of my eyes as I pressed his number on my Favorites.

"I was wondering when you'd get around to calling to tell me you'd almost been killed." Keone's voice was cold.

Dang it. He'd been informed about the attempt to murder me.

"Hey," I said. "I'm okay, though. Thanks for asking."

He said nothing.

"I was shot at last night, as you apparently heard. But I wasn't hit. I had a contingency plan in place at the shack, and it worked. Now I'm in a safe house. How's your day going?"

He still said nothing.

"Um. Banana." I invoked our safe word. Maybe that would get him talking.

Keone exploded. "One thing, Kat! I asked for ONE THING. That you call me and let me know if something big happens to you; that I don't have to hear about it from someone else. But no, that was too much of a commitment! I had to hear it from my cousin, who called me early this morning!"

"It was rude of him to wake you," I fumbled. Truth was, it hadn't crossed my mind to call Mr. K, though I'd remembered to have Pono reach out to Opal and Artie. What was wrong with me? "I didn't want to freak you out," I blustered. "I'm calling now. Everything is fine."

"Everything is not fine. Pono knew I'd want to be called," Keone growled. "Any normal person would understand that I'd want to know if you were safe, especially after the day we had yesterday."

I winced. "I told you I wasn't good at relationships. I've been trying. I remembered the other time—the car accident." A long moment went by. He had to be at work. "Where are you?"

"I'm on break at the Kahului Airport. Between flights." His voice calmed and flattened. "The worst thing is you had to know you were in danger after you listened to that phone call on the Crossbow. Pono told me about it. But I didn't ask about what you heard on the call. On purpose. To respect your professionalism." Keone's voice rose. "And then you let me drop you off and leave you alone at the shack without a word about what you suspected might happen!"

"I didn't want to endanger you," I said. I finally understood why I hadn't said anything to him about Ana's threat. I rubbed my forehead with the heel of my hand. "I'm sorry, Keone."

He ignored my apology. "You didn't tell me you'd heard that the hit was extended to you, but you were worried enough about it to make a cardboard shelter under your shack that ended up saving your life." He blew out a breath. "How do you think that makes me feel?"

"I don't know how it makes you feel." My lips felt numb. I could hardly make them move to form the words. "That's why I said banana."

"I don't think I can do this, Kat."

That sinking feeling in my stomach got worse. I balled a fist and pressed it against my abdomen. "Don't think you can do what?"

"Are you going to make me say it?"

"Yes." My voice was a scratchy whisper.

"You keep saying we're just friends when we both know it's always been more. But it's too stressful, Kat."

"So you won't be friends with me, now?"

"I don't want to hear from someone else that you're dead."

"But how can I call you if I'm dead?"

Keone hung up.

Yeah, I deserved that. Wrong time to be flippant. I stared at the phone in my hand. Wow, a day could go from great to terrible in a few minutes. Wasn't that interesting.

I got up, climbed back in bed, and pulled the covers up over my head.

39

An INDETERMINATE NUMBER of meaningless hours later, a knock woke me.

"Kat. You up?" Muffled voice outside the door.

"Nope." I didn't bother lifting my head from under the covers.

"It's noon, sistah." The bedroom opened with a creak. One odd thing about the treehouse was that there were scarcely any level floors in the place. "We got a call."

Lei's tone put me on alert. I sat up, lowering the blankets and blinking. "Something's happened?"

Lei's brown eyes narrowed, assessing me. "Something's happened to you, too. And I'm not talking about yesterday's near misses." Lei was dressed in her typical detective garb of dark jeans, blue polo shirt, badge on her belt and gun in a shoulder rig. Her curly hair was captured in a haphazard ponytail.

"Oh, ugh." I put my hands over my face and spoke through my fingers. "I don't want to talk about it." My voice was childish.

"Well, I don't have time to play counselor, anyway. Keone called Pono with an alert that a woman matching Ana Davies's description was spotted at the Honolulu Airport in the private plane area. She was accompanied by a well-dressed Asian man. They got on a small aircraft that took off before it could be intercepted. Keone was able to confirm the flight was headed for Hana." She paused as if waiting for a response.

The mention of Keone's name zapped through my whole body like a sore tooth getting probed by a dental drill. I didn't remove my hands from my face.

Lei went on. "Pono and I are going to the Hana airport to check out the lead and see if it's our perp. Stay put, okay?"

"Okay." I kept my face hidden so Lei wouldn't see how a mention of Mr. K had wrecked me.

Lei closed the bedroom door.

I heard the rumble of Pono's bass voice, and then the thump of their feet on the spiral staircase that led from the upper floors in the giant banyan's branches to the lower entrance and living area at ground level.

I flopped back on the pillow and threw an arm over my eyes. "Gah. If this is a broken heart, I'd rather take a bullet." I'd been dumped lots of times due to my touchphobia, but it never felt like this.

I heard the roar of Stanley's engine. The crunch of the tires on the gravel driveway. The creak of the automated gate. The detectives were gone. Silence settled around me.

Well. In a manner of speaking. A mynah landed on the railing and hopped down to *tap tap tap* at something on the deck. I rolled over to watch the bird.

The mynah hopped over to the slider and cocked its head to peer in at me, a bright black eye contrasting with its yellow eyelid and beak. "Squawk!" It spoke. "What did you think was going to happen with this guy, Kat?"

"I hoped it might go better this time," I murmured. Yes, I was anthropomorphizing, but the mynah looked interested and sympathetic.

When the bird flew off, I felt abandoned all over again. I was that nine-year-old girl, alone with the bodies of her parents in a wrecked car. Not that I could remember any of that, thank good-ness. I'd been unconscious, but my body knew the truth of what had happened. My heart did, too. I was always trying to protect myself from another loss like that. Once again it hadn't worked.

I fell asleep, and blessed oblivion shut out my negative thoughts.

~

WHEN I WOKE AGAIN, evening had lengthened the shadows outside the banyan tree house. I was so hungry my "stomach was gnawing on my backbone," as Aunt Fae used to say.

I picked up my phone and checked for messages. No word from Lei or Pono, but a call showed from Edith. She hadn't left a voice-mail. I hit the CALL RETURN button.

"Hello?" Edith answered on the second ring, and though her voice was breathy, my friend sounded like herself again. What a relief.

"Edith! You sound better."

"Kat! Where are you?"

"Out in Hana. How are you? You sound like you've got more energy."

"I'm fine. Sick of being fussed over." I heard a voice in the back-ground. "Josie's here with me, so that's good. I'll put you on speaker and you can say hi."

A moment later Josie's voice said, "Hey, Kat. When are you coming to visit? Edith's getting restless."

I wouldn't tell my elderly friends about the threats I'd had and add stress to their lives about a situation none of us could change. "Not until next weekend at the soonest. I have a real job, you know."

"Well, you're working for me now, too, Sophie tells me," Edith said, satisfaction in her tone.

"Yes, I'm helping with your security detail."

"And since you're out in Hana, maybe you can take care of something there for me."

"Oh yeah?"

"Yeah. On advisement from Josie and other trusted people, including you, I've changed my will. Would you be able to take a copy to Lola at my house and ask her to leave the premises?" A note of unease crept into Edith's voice. "Josie tells me she seems to have a drinking problem."

"Understatement." Josie harrumphed in the background.

"Anyway, if I email you a copy of my new will, could you take it over? And then flex your muscles or something and get her to go." Edith sighed. "It's a big ask, but I don't have what it takes to deal with coming home and finding her there."

I didn't want my friend coming home to that, either. What an utter mess Edith's cottage must be, filled with bits of glass and rubbish, but maybe the police had already ousted Lola. In any case I needed to see what state the house was in. Hopefully Lei and Pono were on their way to capture Ana as we spoke. With Edith providing me a reason and permission to evict Lola, I'd be able to call for police assistance if she gave me any trouble.

"Sure. I can do that. I brought my laptop to where I'm staying. You can email the document to me, and I'll look around and see if there's a printer here." I paused, searching for words. "I know you wanted things to go differently with Lola, Edith. But you need to know she's not in a good place with her drinking. Maybe after she's sober . . ."

"But would Lola be a lush if I'd been there for her? As a mother?" Edith's voice cracked.

"Everyone makes choices, and we live with the consequences." I felt the arrow of that tough truth to my own heart. "You chose to give Lola up for adoption to a family that seemed stable and loving. It was a positive situation for both of you. What happened after that wasn't your fault."

"I'm trying to get there with it." Edith snuffled. Josie murmured comfortingly in the background. "And then there's Ana and how she turned out."

"Some people are just bad apples and should be thrown on the compost heap." I quoted my Aunt Fae on that one. She'd never had time for sugarcoating evil or fools. "Ana is dangerous, and if she's working with the Changs, she's in another category entirely."

A long minute went by. I tossed back the covers and swung my legs out of bed. "Maybe you need a therapist to help you sort things out, Edith."

"Ha!" Edith snorted damply. "I'm too old for head shrinking, thank you very much. But I will listen to trusted friends and colleagues and protect myself from two people who have shown they have no desire for a real reconciliation with me. So if you could help move Lola out and on her way, I'd appreciate it."

"On it." I headed for the bathroom and the shower. "I'll give a call when your house is ready for you to come home to." In the bathroom, I yanked my sleep tee off over my head. "Lei and Pono have a lead on Ana. Hopefully they'll bring her into custody, and the coast will be clear soon for you to return home."

"Thanks, Kat." Edith sounded choked up.

"*Mahalo*," Josie said. "You are real *'ohana* to us."

"Right back at you. Talk soon." I said my goodbyes. My eyes prickled; I was glad I knew that *'ohana* meant family.

I hunted for a jogging bra and fresh exercise clothes in the plastic bag Pono had packed for me. I was on a mission again, and that helped me shake off the conversation with Mr. K.

40

THERE WAS a printer in the house, tucked away in a closet-sized office space downstairs. I checked my email and retrieved the will and printed it.

After that, I foraged in the kitchen (native woods, stainless appliances, and poured cement counters.) I found half a dozen eggs, a couple of yogurts and a small loaf of banana bread in the fridge with a note attached: *Mahalo for staying at the Banyan Tree House. Please review us on Yelp or Tripadvisor and give us five stars if you enjoyed your stay!*

I ate most everything in the fridge, washed down with a pint or so of hot coffee. Never mind that it was close to six p.m. I'd slept the day away and this was breakfast.

Fueled up, fresh from the shower, and dressed in my running clothes, I was ready for action.

I perused my phone. No update calls from Lei and Pono. Nor Mr. K, sadly. I logged into my email. Nothing new since my last check half an hour ago.

I did a map search for Edith's address—less than two miles away, an easy jogging distance from here.

I tried the detectives' phones. They went straight to voicemail.

Staring out the sliders that opened onto the neat lawn bounded by a high fence, I chewed my lip. I was trained to assess this kind of thing. How much danger was I in, really?

I needed to take the attempts on my life seriously—but in my best estimation, I was a secondary target. The attempt to run me off the road had been opportunistic, more of a warning than a real murder attempt.

The shooter last night? Yes. Full serious. But I'd heard them drive off. Even if they staked out my place, they would have lost me after the detectives moved me last night.

Lei and Pono's absence and lack of communication meant they'd likely engaged Ana, their target, and were fully occupied either capturing or booking her. I could safely assume Ana and any partner she had were off the table.

If I made a reasonable effort to conceal my identity and ducked off the road if I saw any large black SUVs, I was probably safe to go on foot to Edith's and evict Lola. I could also call for backup from Hana PD at any point. They were briefed about my situation.

Which left Lola a sitting duck for my mission of bad news and eviction.

I sent Lei a text that I was going to Edith's to deliver news about the will, and kick Lola out per my client's request.

She wouldn't like it, but I was an independent agent with a job to do.

I rubbed my hands together in anticipation. I had an outlet for my bruised emotions. Jogging over to Edith's and kicking Lola out followed by cleaning up the place was the perfect way to get rid of my angst over the breakup with Mr. K.

The sun began to set in the time it took me to jog the narrow back roads of Hana to Edith's little cottage. A full moon rose on one side, orange as a jack-o'-lantern glimpsed between the dimming trees.

I saw no suspicious vehicles, and with a billed hat pulled low, my parka concealing my gun, and sunglasses on, nothing but my height gave me away as Kat Smith, Target of the Mob.

I had to take the glasses off when I got to Edith's long, tree-lined driveway as the light lowered. There was still enough illumination to gild the ferns and trees edging Edith's yard and give good visibility.

I crept toward the cottage, casing the area to make sure Lola didn't have unexpected company. I hung back in the trees near the shed for a visual assessment.

No extra vehicles were parked in the driveway, but I grimaced at the sight of the overflowing trash and fly-buzzing bags of refuse. "Ugh. She still hasn't dealt with the trash."

At least Lola's laundry had disappeared from Edith's vehicle parked in the carport.

I jumped—something had touched me from the shadows.

Butter, Edith's cat, emerged from the ferns as she rubbed her head against my running tights. I squatted to pet her back and felt ribs under her coat. "Has Lola been feeding you, girl?"

Butter purred, winding around my legs. This sweet kitty was a much nicer cat than Tiki, but I missed my semi-feral friend anyway.

A dim light shone from Edith's living room window, and hushed voices reached my ear.

I was glad I'd taken my time on the approach because someone was inside with Lola, or she was on the phone.

"Drat." I hadn't brought the Crossbow device, but I could eavesdrop the old-fashioned way.

I darted across the lawn to the house and slid along the wall, gun drawn, straining to listen through the glass.

41

"HAVE you found those codes yet, Mom?" A woman's youthful voice, one I recognized—Ana! Excitement stirred the hair on my neck. But how had she evaded Lei and Pono?

Didn't matter. This was my opportunity to take her down.

"Edith's got nothing good here. Believe me, I've looked." A woman spoke, slurred and sulky. Lola.

A third voice chilled my blood—the timbre was masculine and cold. "Forget jewelry and knickknacks. We came here to get the passwords to her legal files and accounts. They must be hidden here somewhere."

Adrenaline flooded my veins. The third person had to be Ana's "well-dressed Asian man."

Me against Lola and Ana was a no-brainer, but I was less confident in taking down three perps by myself. However, Lola was already half in the bag and wouldn't put up a fight. That left the other two—and I was armed and had surprise on my side.

I sidled across the porch, grateful that the wooden boards didn't creak as the ones on my porch had when the killer came to my shack.

I tested the front door handle. It was open.

This part was tricky. The screen door opened outward because of the inner main one, which had to be opened inward in the opposite direction.

I'd have to be fast when I committed to action.

I mentally plotted my moves, glad that I was familiar with the layout of the house and the likely positions of the perps in the living room.

I took a deep breath, rolled my eyes heavenward, called upon Good Orderly Direction (also known as God) and leapt forward.

I shoved the screen door open, swung into the opening with my gun held two-handed, and aimed a kick at the handle of the front panel. The barrier flew back to hit the wall inside, and I jumped in, weapon ready. "Freeze! Hands where I can see them."

Lola shrieked, hands flying up in the air from her position on the recliner. Two people across from her spun toward me, eyes wide. A striking man with shoulder-length, bleached blond hair growled and reached for his waistband as the woman glared, hatred twisting her pretty features. "You're supposed to be dead!"

I fixed my aim on the man who was going for his gun. "Leave it. You're not faster than a bullet. Move away from Lola. Both of you against the far wall."

Grudgingly, Ana and her companion complied, stepping backward to stand against an empty wall. I kept my weapon on them, senses on high alert as we faced off in the dim room. Only the glow of the table lamp illuminated our standoff.

I scanned for something to restrain the two with and couldn't see anything handy.

Dang it, I should have thought of that!

But I could probably hold them where they were until the cops arrived. I fumbled my phone out of my pocket, keeping the gun on Ana and the man as I tried to scroll to the 911 function with a thumb.

Lola pulled the lever on the recliner and her feet hit the floor. "What're you doing, Kat?"

"I'm taking these two into custody. Stay where you are."

Lola didn't obey. She wallowed to standing. "I don't want you to hurt Ana," she said.

"I won't unless she does something stupid." It was hard to keep one eye on Ana and her partner, and the other on Lola. In fact, it was impossible. "Lola! Get back in the chair!"

"No." Lola pulled a huge gold-plated pistol out of a pocket in her caftan. I knew that kind of gun. It weighed a ton and had the kick of an ostrich. "Drop your gun, Kat," she said.

Rats! It never paid to underestimate a hostile, and I'd seriously done so with Lola. "No way. That isn't hap—"

Lola fired, cutting me off.

The boom of her weapon was deafening. For a minute, I wasn't sure if I'd been shot because the sound felt like a blow. I recoiled instinctively, stumbling backward and banging into a side table.

No, I hadn't been shot, but now there was a huge hole in the wall next to where my head had been.

Ana dove for the floor as the man pulled his gun and spun to face me.

I steadied my aim on him and employed my loudest, most authoritative commanding voice. "Both of you, drop your weapons!"

The recoil from Lola's shot had thrown the woman back into the recliner. Watching her flop about, waving the golden gun and moaning aloud from the noise and the kick would've been funny if it hadn't been so dangerous. "No way, Kat. You drop your gun. I'll get you the next time."

I had my weapon trained on Ana's partner. Despite Lola's near miss, he still seemed more dangerous to me. Trouble was, now the dude had the business end of a Glock pointed my way. "Give it up, Kat. You're outnumbered."

"We are not on a first name basis, Mister . . . ?"

"None of your business."

"This here's Fabio Chang," Lola said, "and he's got major connections, so you better listen to him, missy."

"Mo-ther!" Ana cried petulantly. "We're trying to keep his name out of all of this!"

"And now you know it." Fabio narrowed his eyes and swung the Glock up just a hair—he meant business. "Drop your weapon and kick it over to me."

Sweat broke out on my forehead.

I'd lost my two advantages, surprise and being the only one with a gun. Now I was facing two—no, THREE people with weapons pointed my way, because Ana had pulled a baby two-shot revolver out of an ankle holster while she was down on the ground. She rolled on her side and pointed it at me.

There was no physical way I could shoot all three, positioned where they were, without being pumped full of lead myself.

"Let's make a deal," I said. "I already called the cops. This island won't be big enough to hide from the heat that killing me will bring down."

"We've been fine staying under their radar so far," Fabio said. "I'll take that risk." His eyes were a snake's—dark, glittery, and hard to read.

Ana frowned, though. "What are you offering?"

"I'll surrender my weapon. You can restrain me and make a getaway."

"That sounds good." Lola hauled herself out of the recliner at last. Her arm sagged with the weight of the revolver, and she hoisted it aloft with both hands. "Or maybe I'll just shoot you."

And then she did.

42

I came around to discover my face squashed onto the carpet. Someone was tying my hands behind my back with cord—not gently, either.

I played possum to see what the heck had happened and how badly I'd been hurt. As if in answer, my head began to thump.

"I can't believe you tried to shoot her, Mom," Ana's voice came from somewhere off to the left. "Twice. Didn't know you had it in you."

"The first time I wanted to scare her. The second . . . I di-didn't mean to. My finger slipped." Lola's voice wobbled.

"Maybe that's why you missed. For the second time," Fabio Chang said from above me. "Good thing she jumped back, tripped over the side table and knocked herself out."

Oh son of a groundhog, was that what happened? I grimaced in embarrassment.

"At least it ended the standoff." Fabio tightened the final knot. "Kat might have been bluffing about calling the cops—it didn't seem like she completed her 911 call. We should get out of here, though, because she probably texted her friends about where she was going. We can take her with us, keep her as a hostage if we run into trouble."

"Sounds good," Ana said.

Lola began to cry. "I didn't mean any of this to happen! My mother's house is wrecked. I can't leave it like this," she snuffled.

"You can and you will. Let's go, Mom." The sound of their lumbering footsteps passed by.

Fabio slapped my exposed cheek. "Wakey wakey."

"Ugh," I said, spitting out rug fibers. "My head hurts."

"You whacked yourself on the wall. Good going, Agent Smith. Real smooth."

"You're not a nice person."

He yanked my bound arms in reply, surprising a yelp of pain out of me. "Let's get moving."

My best strategy at this point was to slow the suspects, giving Lei and Pono time to respond to my text and check on Edith's house. I spotted my phone on the floor, partly hidden by my body. I had to either get it or hide it—but my arms bound behind my back made retrieving it unlikely. "I can't move my legs."

Fabio kicked me in the thigh—not too hard, but hard enough.

"Ow!" I moved my legs after that, all right. I flopped around and managed to kick the phone under the side table that knocked me over. Hopefully Lei or Pono would find it and know I'd been here, and something was very wrong.

Ana returned. The smell of Lola's old pizza boxes stacked against the wall wafted around us as the two of them half-shoved, half-carried me down the shadowy hall toward Edith's back door. I let my head loll against Ana's shoulder, leaning heavily on her and dragging my feet.

"Holy cannoli, she really is a giant," Ana huffed.

"Quit wasting your breath. Let's get her secured in the car," Fabio said.

Outside, the grove of guava trees surrounding the backyard swayed in the night breeze, casting flickering moonlight patterns over the grass. The pair hauled me roughly over uneven ground toward another carport, not visible from the front of the house, where the big black SUV that had been my nemesis was parked. Had Ana and Chang been the ones trying to kill me?

It seemed so.

Lola was waiting beside the vehicle. The side passenger door was open, and the interior light gleamed on her long fake nails and worried face as she twisted her hands. "Where should we put her?"

"In the back," Chang panted.

Lola hustled around and opened the cargo door at the rear of the vehicle. Chang and Ana pushed me inside. Chang whipped the belt out of his pants and captured my legs in spite of my kicking, binding them together with the leather strap. "That ought to hold you for the moment."

"You don't think you can get away with this, do you?" Being driven somewhere by people with murder on their minds is not recommended. I was starting to get worried.

"That's another thing we need to take care of," Chang said. "Your big mouth." He picked up a beach towel from the floor of the vehicle and, using a combat knife of impressive dimensions, cut a slit in the side of it and ripped off a strip.

I fought full on at that point, but with Ana holding my lower body down and Chang smothering me with the towel until I opened my mouth, I was soon gagged as well as restrained.

"I'm feeling uncomfortable with this whole situation," Lola said suddenly. "I think I'll go inside and have a drink."

"No, Mom!" Ana yelled. "The cops will come here as soon as they realize she's missing!"

"So? I'll tell them Kat never arrived."

"And those bullet holes in the walls?" Chang asked.

"The place is a mess already. I'll say she never showed up, and that I was shooting at creepy crawlies coming out of the wood-work." Lola belched. "They'll believe me. I can be very convincing."

That was true. I'd dismissed her as a hapless drunk myself. A chill passed over me, raising the hair on my arms.

"Okay, Mom, whatever. Keep looking for those codes and call me when you have them," Ana said. "When we're secure we'll send for you to join us."

The vehicle dipped as my captors climbed in. Doors slammed, trapping me in darkness. The engine roared, jolting forward. I rolled helplessly with each swerving turn Fabio made until I braced myself against the violent motion by wedging my feet into a corner. Edith's beloved cottage disappeared behind us, and the reality of my abduction sank like a stone in my gut.

I tried to stand alone against the shadows. Now, they engulfed me.

Not that I was being dramatic or anything—but being bound, gagged, and taken by force in a vehicle seldom ended well for the victim.

The vehicle turned onto the main road and hung a right.

Ah, they were heading toward Ohia. I tuned my senses, absorbing clues and mentally picturing a route that had become familiar. The moist smell of rotting mangoes filtered through the air vents—we must be in the rainforest.

The turns were abrupt, and Fabio was taking them fast. I slid back and forth, unable to brace myself well enough to keep from being flung around. We eventually bounced over what felt like a cattle guard, then the road became rough.

We'd passed Ohia and were on the "backside" of the island—I recognized the pattern.

The binding around my wrists irritated them. I wriggled my fingers to keep circulation going and flexed my feet to do the same.

The warm organic smell of cow wafted in as the SUV slowed and turned. We lurched down a steep decline, likely a valley. The grassy scent intensified—we were passing through farmland. The SUV slowed and we bumped along a rocky gravel road.

I lost my ability to mentally map where I was, so I focused on resting and conserving strength, breathing deep and flexing my limbs to keep my circulation going.

At last we halted, and the doors opened. A familiar sound pierced the air—the high-pitched, frenzied yapping of a small dog. I recognized the voice of Sassy, Pua's toy poodle.

Understanding crystallized like an icicle trailing down my spine. They'd brought me all the way to Pua Chang's remote homestead, probably to dispose of me where my body would be hard to find.

43

THE YAPPING INTENSIFIED to deafening and shrill as the back door of the SUV was opened. "Down, Sassy! Hush now!" Pua's gentle scolding reached my ears, but the dog's barking overshadowed the conversation.

Then Pua saw who was in the back of the SUV.

"What were you thinking?" She kept her tone soft, but tension thrummed beneath. "How did this happen?"

"Kat caught us at Edith's." Ana's icy voice. "We're finishing what we started. Tonight, the thorn in our side gets removed for good."

A prickle of fear tightened my skin. They couldn't mean . . . surely Pua wouldn't allow it. I had to find a way to communicate, seek her help. But for now, bound and gagged, I could only listen and wait.

Rough hands jostled me as I was hefted over a broad shoulder and carried up creaking steps. My position gave me a prime view of Chang's backside, straining at the seams of his tight designer jeans.

"Ugh," I mumbled into my gag, wriggling helplessly.

I was dumped onto cushions that reeked of dog inside the dimly lit mudroom of Pua's house.

I peeked through slitted eyes, glimpsing Pua holding Sassy like a fuzzy white football in the background, as the conspirators stared at me.

"I don't appreciate you bringing this trouble to my doorstep, Cousin," Pua said sourly. "I'm already in enough legal hot water."

"You're family. You have to help," Chang stated. What an arrogant jerk!

Pua rolled her eyes. "Well, what do you want me to do, then?"

"Help us get rid of her somewhere the body won't be found," Chang said.

Just as I suspected! I suppressed a shiver and glared defiantly at them instead. "Yoll neff geth afway wif dis," I yelled through the gag.

But the odds were good that they would get away with it. A body could lie a long time out here without discovery, as I already knew.

Fabio Chang managed to look stylish even with half-circles of sweat under the arms of his designer silk shirt. Hands on hips, expression unhappy, he turned to Pua.

"After we get rid of this problem," he nudged me with the toe of a snakeskin shoe, "Ana and I need to get moving. The New Ohia operation is now in the hands of the FBI and we're in damage control mode. They picked up our manager Thompkins, and he's likely to tell all in return for a deal. They also shut down our U.S. assets, but we've still got most of the money in offshore accounts. We'll kick some back to you for your help. We want to take your car to where we have our private plane stashed. This ride is too hot."

So that's how they'd sneaked by Lei and Pono . . . they'd landed somewhere else! I wanted to hear more. Was the big black vehicle, a.k.a. BBB, the one that had chased me off the road?

"What's wrong with your ride?" Pua asked, right on cue.

"The SUV was used by one of our men to try to get rid of Edith and this one." Fabio toed me again. He seemed to like doing that. "The killer failed with both targets, so I fired him—but the cops have the vehicle's description and are looking for it."

"I see." Pua stroked Sassy, her eyes concerned. "So. My cut for helping. How much are we talking?"

I couldn't stifle a gasp—was my erstwhile friend going to help murder me?

Fabio raised a brow. "How does two million sound?"

"Make it three."

"Done."

I squeaked like a stepped-on chew toy, all the expression the gag would allow.

Pua pointed to a nearby garden shed. "There's a wheelbarrow, plastic bags, and a shovel in there. I don't want any blood or trace near the house. I have a good spot in mind. You can put her in the barrow, and I'll take you there."

Fabio moved off, but Ana stayed behind. "Get us some food and drinks for the road," she barked at Pua. "I get grumpy when I'm hungry."

Pua frowned. "Get it yourself. The kitchen is that way."

"I want to keep an eye on the prisoner. I don't trust you," Ana said.

My heart sank into my Nikes. Maybe Pua had been looking for a chance to talk to me alone, but it wasn't to be.

"For three mil, I can pack a few sandwiches." Pua walked off, carrying Sassy into the house. A thick silence descended as the door clicked shut behind them.

"I'll finally be rid of you." Ana spun her little silver derringer like a cowgirl in a bad Western. "I've been wanting to take you out since the courthouse steps when you messed up my plan to nail my grandma once and for all."

I gestured to the gag. I had a few things to say to her.

Ana scowled. "No. I don't want your mind games messing up my concentration."

But Ana'd want to hear me beg; I was certain of that. The little psychopath was well-matched with her evil partner Fabio Chang.

I squinted my eyes shut and let myself feel how sad I was about

Mr. K breaking up with me.

It didn't take two seconds for weeping I'd been holding back all day to flood my eyes. I snuffled pitifully, snot clogging my nose, and turned my head to wipe my face on my shoulder.

The tears came faster as I let myself picture Aunt Fae's face when she found out I'd been killed. Opal and Artie would probably have a wake for me on the porch of the general store with all the Red Hat ladies. That would be something to miss.

But I really got going when I imagined Tiki wandering around the jungle and the shack, meowing as she searched for me.

Sobs racked my body and I struggled to breathe.

Yeah, I had feelings all right. I loved my life in Ohia, I wasn't ready for it to be over, and I even had a few people and a feline who'd care that I was gone.

"Oh for crying out loud. You're a poor excuse for a federal agent. No wonder they reassigned you out here in the middle of nowhere." Ana yanked the gag out of my mouth, so the wet rag hung around my neck. "You're slobbering all over yourself."

"I don't wanna die!" I wailed with perfect truth. "Oh please, why do I have to die?"

"Because . . ." Ana paused, a frown creasing her forehead. "Because you're in the way and always have been."

"How am I in the way?" I wiped my streaming eyes on my shoulder again. "Yeah, it was my job to protect Edith. I work for Security Solutions and Edith hired us for protection. But I'll quit. Consider me off the case, as of now."

Ana shook her head. "Nope. Not good enough."

"You know too much and you're dangerous to the Chang interests here in Ohia." Fabio came back at that moment, carrying a shovel and a roll of garbage bags. "Plus, I don't like you." He tossed out a swath of black plastic bags onto the floor. He raised the shovel overhead, business end up. "Ana, let's move her onto the plastic. We can do it right here. She'll be easier to transport when she isn't resisting."

44

"PUA! PUA, HELP!" I bellowed. My (possibly, hopefully) savior appeared, carrying an old-fashioned wicker picnic basket. Trust Pua to pack a picnic all Martha Stewart-style, no matter the situation.

She took one look at the scene and clicked her tongue. "I told you, Fabio. Not here. You don't think blood will fly all over if you whack her with the shovel?" Pua held up her own revolver, a snub-nosed Colt. "I have an unregistered gun for situations like this. Get her into the wheelbarrow and we'll move her to the spot I have picked out and you can be on your way. I'll shoot her and dispose of her myself, but I want you off my land, ASAP."

"What about the SUV?" Fabio said.

"I think I can get away with the SUV being ditched here and you stealing my car since I leave the keys inside it," Pua said. "But I don't want any trace you were ever here beyond that. Seriously, the cops are all over me."

Ana and Fabio exchanged a glance. "For that I'll throw in fifty grand so you can buy a new car to replace the one we're taking," Fabio said. "More than generous."

"Fine," Pua said.

The two wasted no time lifting me, struggling against my bonds like a caterpillar stuck in its cocoon, up off the dog bed couch to the wheelbarrow Fabio had fetched from the garden shed. Pua lined the barrow with plastic bags so no trace from my body sullied its clean metal surface, and they forced me into it.

After handing Ana and Fabio each a headlamp, Pua led the way while Sassy remained in the house, barking her head off. The former postal clerk held a flashlight, though the moon was now bright enough to illuminate a dirt footpath leading behind the ranch house.

Fabio put muscle into hefting me and the wheelbarrow along the trail with Ana's help to get over lumps and bumps. The trail headed up an incline which I hoped got steeper and more difficult. Anything to slow this literal death march.

"What are you two going to do about Lola?" I asked, taking advantage of the gag being off. "I'm guessing you thought you'd kill Edith and she'd inherit, but now that's fallen apart."

"Mom's on her own," Ana panted, helping Fabio heave the wheelbarrow over a rock in the trail. "She's got good survival instincts, and I've got a new partner now." She managed to make googly eyes at Fabio as they each held a handle of the barrow.

"Hm. I'd be worried about how much she might say about your operation in return for immunity." I adjusted my long legs so they were slightly less uncomfortable.

"She doesn't know anything important," Ana said. "I made sure of that. Now that she's not going to inherit from Edith, she's no use to me."

"Good, because I wasn't going to let Lola join us where we're going, anyway," Fabio said. "Was glad she opted to stay behind. Saved getting rid of her later."

"I know." Ana batted her eyes, and Fabio leaned over to kiss her.

What a pair! I gagged, turning it into a cough.

Pua made a rude noise from up ahead. "You two may be ready to take my car and the picnic basket and get on with your lives, but

I still have to clean up your mess and I'd just as soon get it over with."

I shut my eyes, curling into myself, conserving my strength. Hopefully I'd have a last chance to turn the tables before the end.

Ana and Fabio both had to work hard to get me up a slope and I hoped it wore them out. "How much further?" Ana huffed.

"Here," Pua said. They dropped the barrow. "Come see."

They walked around the equipage and went to investigate what Pua was showing them.

I opened my eyes and gazed up at a vividly starry sky embellished by the bright moon that had risen while I jogged to Edith's house what seemed like days ago.

We were on a rise, and from where the wheelbarrow had come to a halt, I could see all the way down the canyon where Pua lived to the ocean, sparkling black and silver. A gentle breeze cooled my hot, wet cheeks. If I shut my eyes, I could imagine the wind was my guardian angel, whisking the tears off my cheeks.

Yes, I'd try hard to survive but there was a good possibility that Pua was going to kill me. Three million dollars was a big incentive. She'd be able to explain away the SUV and her car, and as long as they never found my body, she could get away with murder. She had a great lawyer who would paint her as a victim of her criminal family while making sure none of the Changs were ever named.

"That hiding spot will do nicely," Fabio said to Pua as the trio returned. "No one will ever find her in that volcanic fissure."

"I told you it would work." Pua and Ana fussed with the plastic bags, spreading them out beside the wheelbarrow.

Bam!

Fabio flipped the wheelbarrow to the side, and I fell out onto the hard ground, the breath knocked out of me. "Roll her over and get her facedown on top of these. I'll shoot her, and after I bag the body, I'll roll her into the crack I showed you."

"You got it." New energy crackled between Ana and Fabio. Whatever she'd showed them must have been convincing. Dread curdled my stomach. I thrashed and fought, to no avail. Soon I was positioned for death atop the plastic bags, Ana holding me down with a foot in my lower back.

"But before you go, I need that money you promised me." Pua raised her gun and her flashlight. It shone in their eyes, blinding as a pro. Ana and Fabio had put their weapons away to deal with moving me, so she had the drop on them. "Use your phone and transfer the money to me now."

"No way. We'll call you from the road," Fabio said. "We'll move the money wherever you want once we're safe."

Off in the distance but getting louder, the sound of sirens ululated over the landscape and reached our ears.

Ana and Fabio whirled to look back down the valley. A string of flashing red and blue lights were heading up the narrow road toward Pua's house. "Cops!" Ana yelled.

"You double-crossed us!" Fabio railed.

"I would never," Pua said with dignity, holding her gun steady on them. "I'm a Chang. The cops must have figured out where you were taking her on their own. I can still kill her and get rid of the body like we talked about. They'll have a hard time getting anything to stick to you. But I want my money now."

"Fabio! We can run from here," Ana cried. "We don't have to take Pua's car. We can leave now and get away cross-country."

Fabio ignored this, focusing on Pua. "I'm not giving you anything until we're safely away from here."

A short pause as the three criminals considered their impasse. Meanwhile, I savored each precious breath.

"Fine. As a good faith gesture, give me the offshore account numbers and I'll hold them for you in case you're taken," Pua said.

"You can't get into them without the access codes, anyway, and I've got those up here." Fabio tapped his temple. "But you're right. I don't want the cops getting the account numbers." He pulled out his wallet and took a slip of paper out of it, handing it to Pua. "Keep these safe and I'll reach out to you when we're free. You'll get your payment then."

"That's acceptable," Pua said. She lowered her gun.

"Let's go, Ana." Fabio grabbed Ana's hand. The two hurried off into the wild Maui dark, their headlamps bobbing.

A long, thick silence, broken only by the sound of oncoming sirens off in the distance, settled over Pua and me. I shut my eyes and braced myself, saying mental goodbyes to everyone I loved.

It was a short list—and Keone Kaihale's name was on it. What a moment to realize I'd fallen in love despite my best efforts not to.

I couldn't stifle a big, wet sob. "Just do it already," I choked out. "I can't stand the suspense anymore, Pua."

45

Pua patted my arm. "I wasn't going to shoot you, Kat. Not unless I had to put a bullet in you to make it look real. Sorry for the stress." She dropped to her knees beside me, setting down her gun and the flashlight. "Glad that worked and they're gone. Thought the cops would never get here."

She opened a slim Swiss Army knife procured from a pocket and sawed at the rope binding my arms.

My numb limbs fell to my sides as the ropes released. Still face-down on plastic, the reprieve of my death sentence took a bit to sink in as tingles of returning circulation prickled my extremities.

Pua went to work on the belt around my legs. "The police should be able to pick those two up now that they're on foot."

I turned my head to address her. "You could've given me a clue."

"No, I couldn't. It was worth it to try to get my money, but I at least wanted those account numbers for the FBI so they could seize the New Ohia assets. Fabio had to believe I was on his side." Pua grabbed me by the arm and gave a tug. "On your feet, my friend. Let's go meet the police."

～

ONCE AGAIN, I was wrapped in a blanket, but this time it was one of Pua's soft Hawaiian-style quilts. I held a mug of hot soup that had been simmering all day in her Crock-Pot and sipped it gingerly. Sassy finally decided I was okay. She leaned her quivery, nervous little body against me as I sat on her doggy couch in the mudroom.

In the living area of her house, Pua was giving her statement to Lei, Pono, and a couple of first responders who'd come to answer the 911 call she made when Fabio, Ana and I first arrived.

I would give my statement next.

The physical relief of being safe, warm, and having something in my belly caught up with me. I slid over to the side and fell asleep.

A BRUSH of fingers on my forehead, moving the hair out of my eyes, woke me.

I didn't lash out this time.

I was safe and this person was gentle—someone who cared about me. I could feel it in the soft way those fingers caressed my hair.

I opened my eyes and gazed into Keone's concerned brown ones.

"Hello." My voice cracked. The yelling, crying, and gag did a number on my throat.

"Hello." His fingers smoothed my hair back again, then curved around to cup my cheek. "Are you okay?"

"Yep." But then I remembered he'd broken up with me and my eyes filled. "Nope."

"Can I hug you?"

I nodded.

He sat beside me—Sassy was gone—and drew me into his arms, blanket and all. "You didn't hit me when I woke you up."

I sighed, relaxing against him. "I told you I was trying."

"I know you did."

"How are you here? All the way out at Pua's?"

"Pono called me. He knew I'd want to come."

I leaned into his hug, listening to the thump of his heart— slightly faster than usual—and oh, how good it felt to be there.

Lei stuck her head around the doorframe. "Hey, you guys. Kat needs to give her statement to us privately. Keone, would you mind joining Pua in the kitchen? She's got some nice soup and it's hot."

I pointed to the empty mug at my feet. "I can vouch for the soup."

"I'll wait with Pua and take you home after you're done with the police," Keone told me.

My eyes prickled again. "Thanks. That would be great."

He left for the kitchen, and Lei and Pono waited until I moved in and settled myself on Pua's living room couch.

All the doors were closed. Lei took her phone recorder out and set it on the coffee table. "I'll record your statement in a moment, but first we wanted to update you."

"Yes please." I made prayer hands.

"First of all, we sent the uniforms we arrived with out looking for the two suspects," Lei said. "Though we're not too hopeful about finding them in the dark, with a head start."

"Be better to focus on roadblocks and wherever they landed that private plane," I volunteered. "What's been going on? Where were you two all day?"

Pono shook his finger at me in a scolding way. "Don't try to get out of the fact that you left the safe house and went on your own to Edith's. Look how that turned out!"

"Turned out fine," I defended. "Though I'll admit it wouldn't have if Pua hadn't turned on Ana and Fabio and saved the day."

Lei pinched the bridge of her nose. "Let's retrace our steps a bit and we'll start at the beginning from our end. We left you with strict instructions to stay at the safe house."

"Yes, but—"

"You'll get your turn," she told me severely. "We went to the Hana Airport, following up on Keone's tip that he saw a couple matching the suspects' descriptions boarding a private plane, yada yada you know all that. Well, we sat around and waited, but that flight never arrived within the time frame it should have. We were tracking down where it might have gone when we got a 911 call about a body."

My eyes flew wide. "A body? Whose?"

"We didn't know anything except that it was a male in his mid-thirties, mixed-race. We went out to a remote location in the Hana area with no phone reception, a hidden landing strip. The plane was gone, but that's probably where they landed. Anyway, we were investigating the corpse, with all the protocols that entails, when I eventually got your text saying you were going to Edith's to roust Lola."

I cringed. "Ah." In hindsight my thought process at the time didn't make a ton of sense. "I was eager to kick her out and clean the place up."

"Kat, that wasn't your job." Pono rubbed his big hands together in a circular motion, as if wanting to choke someone.

"Well, it kind of was since Edith hired Security Solutions and by extension, me. And when my client called and asked me to tell Lola about her will and asked me to get the woman out of there, I chose to obey."

Pono rolled his eyes heavenward and smacked his thighs with a sound like a pistol shot. Clearly, he wasn't happy with me.

Lei went on. "We didn't think your side trip to Edith's was an emergency until we found the dead guy's weapon tossed in the bushes. A quick check showed that the slugs inside matched the caliber of the those we'd retrieved from the wall behind your bed."

I opened my mouth and then shut it.

"At that point, we realized he was the assassin who'd made an attempt on Edith and you. The guy had been executed, and the black SUV you'd described was missing and thus in play." Lei narrowed her eyes at me. "And the most likely place for Ana Davies to have gone, if she was involved, was Edith's."

"The guy whose body you found. The assassin failed, and he was fired," I said. "That's what Fabio Chang said."

"Yep, 'fired' is one way to put it. He'd been killed with his own gun," Lei said. "Once we put that together, we zoomed over to Edith's, lights and sirens off, hoping to surprise whoever might be at the house." She fiddled with the white bone hook I'd seen her play with before, rubbing it between her fingers as she eyed me. "And what do you think we found there?" She was clearly as miffed as Pono was.

"I didn't expect those two to be with Lola when I got there. They'd hidden the SUV in back," I said.

Both detectives were stony-faced. "This is where you tell us what happened," Pono said. "Officially, and for the record."

"I'd prefer if you told me what you found when you got there, first. I'm curious." Truth was, I was mortified I'd let that lame threesome get the better of me.

"Nope. You go next," Lei said while Pono made that unnerving twisting movement with his hands. "We're recording now." She pushed the ON button.

"Okay, okay." I described the events at Edith's from my point of view, all the way up to being driven away in the BBB. "I kicked my phone under the side table, so you'd know I'd been there," I said. "Lola turned out to be the dark horse, discharging her weapon twice. I'd underestimated her. But I hoped you'd find my phone and know that whatever Lola said, I'd been there and had been taken against my will."

Lei asked a few clarifying questions, and then turned off the recording.

"Okay, here's what happened for us. We left our vehicle down the driveway to approach quietly on foot. A light was on, so we sneaked up on the porch, and the door opened. It wasn't even shut all the way," Lei said. "Lola was passed out in the recliner. After we poked around and found her spent brass, her gun, the holes in the wall and your phone, Pono woke her up. He's the good cop." She smiled and showed her pointy canines.

I shivered. "Then what?"

"We poked holes in her story until she broke down," Pono said. "Turns out she didn't know where Fabio and Ana were headed. But when the 911 dispatch got a call from Pua's, we were at the head of the charge. We'd already planned to go to Pua's place next because of her family connection to the Changs."

"All's well that ends well," I said, rubbing my chafed wrists. "Pua saved the day by faking out Ana and Fabio that she was going to kill me and hide my body."

Lei turned on the recorder again, and I finished my story with what went down since I arrived at Pua's. "She deserves a medal. She turned down three million dollars to save my life."

The two detectives exchanged a glance. "We'll be sure to pass it along to the District Attorney prosecuting her case," Pono said. "Now, where are those account codes?"

"Pua has them. On a slip of paper Fabio gave her," I said.

"She says she gave them to you," Lei replied. "Up until this detail, your stories matched."

My eyes opened wide. "Uh-oh."

And wasn't that an understatement.

46

PUA AND KEONE were seated on stools at the breakfast bar in her pristine, marble-floored kitchen, spooning up soup, when I entered followed by Lei and Pono.

"Hey, Kat. You're looking better," Pua said upon seeing me.

"Thanks," I said. "For everything. Except that last bit about how you gave me the account numbers. You did not."

Pua was unfazed. "Sorry if that made you uncomfortable, but it's my only leverage and I didn't want to deal with that aspect until we'd both had a break." She indicated the steaming pot on the stove. "Detectives, want some soup?"

"We haven't had dinner," Pono said, taking a bowl from the stack on the counter. "So I don't mind if I do." He ladled himself a large helping. "Minestrone. Yum."

Lei trained hot laser eyes on Pua. She put her hands on her hips. "I'm calling the FBI about this."

"Good. I want them on board. The DA's office too," Pua said. "Detective Kaihale, there's fresh bread in the box if you'd like some."

Pono opened a modern marble breadbox on the counter and

took out a crusty loaf. He ripped off a large piece. "How do you have such good food way out here?"

"Cooking with fresh produce I've grown is one of my hobbies, and baking bread is soothing. I have a lot of time on my hands since I was fired from the post office." She dipped a bit of bread in her soup. "It's a pleasure to feed people."

Pua seemed to mean it, and I was still hungry, so I got in line behind Pono with an empty bowl and a chunk of bread in hand.

"Where are those codes, Pua?" Lei said.

Pua set her spoon down and sighed. "You've got no criminal charges on me for the current situation since I did nothing but try to help Kat. So, I've been thinking that I'll offer to exchange the codes for an immunity deal on my other case. I want my old job at the post office back."

My heart lifted. I'd love to have Pua back in the post office, working with me.

But Lei snorted. "You were arrested for drug trafficking through the postal service! That's grounds for dismissal to say the least."

"I was framed by some elements in the family who haven't liked my independence. No one has listened to me on that but my lawyer. Thankfully, the case is falling apart for lack of evidence, and I expect the charges to be dismissed soon." Pua dabbed her mouth with a napkin. "I'm willing to overlook how I've been treated and offer you the overseas access codes in return for dropping all charges against me and reinstating me to my job. With the account numbers and a court order, the FBI can freeze those assets. Trust me—they're going to want to. If Fabio was willing to pay me three million, how much more do you guess are in those accounts?"

Lei fumed for a moment, then spun on a heel and headed for the door. "I'm going to make some calls. None of you go anywhere."

Pono followed her, carrying his full bowl with a chunk of bread floating in the broth. "Stay put," he said through a mouthful. "All of you." He grabbed the rest of Pua's fresh bread on his way out.

The three of us glanced at each other, then commenced eating. When my soup was gone, I set my spoon aside. "Well-played, Pua."

She gave a delicate shrug. "I'm trying to make the best of a tough situation." Sassy, at her feet, gave a supportive yap.

"I wouldn't be surprised if you get all you're asking for," Keone said, carrying his bowl to the sink. "Especially if your case was going to be hard to prosecute."

I agreed. It was likely she was going to get her deal. I had a good rapport with our Head Postmaster, Mr. Hanoi, and I was pretty sure a word from me would help her get her job back. But I had to lay down a boundary. "As current Ohia Postmaster, I insist that you don't run any drugs through the post office in the future," I said, trying for a stern tone as I slurped my soup.

"I was framed," Pua repeated. "I can't discuss it beyond that. But there are elements in the family that don't like me, as I told the detectives."

"And there will be more of those when they find out you flipped on Ana and Fabio," I said, with concern. "Are you going to be okay? Safe?"

"Yes. Because I have Terence's backing." Pua smiled. "In fact, he warned me Fabio might drop by and demand I help. He suggested I try to get the codes and use them to bargain."

"That's good news. I guess." I was still unclear how much we could trust someone like Terence Chang, but that was above my pay grade. "Meanwhile, I know a couple of little girls who can't wait for you to get back behind the counter."

"Sandy and Windy?" Pua perked up. "How are they doing?"

"Not so great, to be honest. They're looking unkempt and I think the family was out of food. We took care of it, though." I told Pua about my recent confrontation with the girls and my efforts to bribe their friendship. "Windy doesn't like me. She has her sights set on marrying Keone."

Mr. K returned to sit beside me. He muttered something unintelligible, his ears turning red.

"What's that?" I elbowed him.

"I went by their house a few times and fixed things when I was going out with their auntie Lani. Maybe that's what caused it," he mumbled.

My eyebrows shot up as I thought of the pretty young woman who'd waited on Sophie and me at the hotel. "Wow. That makes sense. Are you . . .?"

"No, we're not going out anymore. That was months ago," he snapped. "Before you came to Maui."

"That's fine. None of my business. Since you broke up with me, anyway."

Our eyes locked for a long, hot moment.

"Ahem." Pua stood up, reaching for my empty bowl. "You said something about taking Kat home tonight, Keone? Maybe you two should take this somewhere private."

"Yes," Mr. K said. "Let's do that. I'm pretty sure the detectives are done with Kat, but I'll go see." He left abruptly.

Pua turned on the sink, one of those deep steel double-sided numbers. Though she had a dishwasher, she squirted soap into one basin and filled it with bubbles.

I closed the breadbox and cleaned up the rest of the items left on the breakfast bar: a soup ladle, small plates, and a butter knife or two. I brought the dishes and handed them to Pua. She rinsed them and submerged them in suds.

I moved in next to her and rinsed the dishes she handed me, stacking them in the drainer. We worked side by side, silent and companionable. When we were done, she dried her hands on a towel and glanced around to make sure the room was empty.

She turned and spoke in a low voice. "I'm calling Terence in case Fabio and Ana get away from the police. I believe he'll want to make sure they're disciplined for all the ways they messed up New Ohia Vision and ruined the place for the family."

I had nothing to say so I nodded.

"I'll let you know what I find out about what's going to happen with New Ohia," she went on. "My guess is that the land will revert to the state. People who bought lots will be compensated with what is regained but will likely lose their money."

"They had too much of it anyway if they were buying up future houses in a shady development with cash," I said.

Pua shrugged. "Other than being sad it won't be a family retreat like I hoped, I'm glad New Ohia's shut down."

"Me too."

She cocked her head. "But there will still be a couple of empty model homes left there. Maybe you want to live in one and be a caretaker or something?"

"Maybe," I said. "No way to tell what's going to happen."

A little smile lurked around Pua's mouth. "We'll see. I know people." She handed me a sponge. "Can you wipe the counters? I'm going to scrub the stove."

I took the sponge and went to do her bidding.

I loved my little shack, but it sure would be nice not to have to worry about break-ins or Miss Prissy jumping on my head while I was asleep. Still, living in one of those fancy model homes was a big step up for a humble civil servant. I wouldn't get my hopes up.

Keone returned as I was putting the sponge away in a neat holder on the dish drainer. "C'mon, Kat. They're done with you for today. They still want to meet with Pua, though. Things seem to be moving ahead with the D.A."

"Oh good." I embraced Pua quickly, before my touchphobia could get going. Her return hug was light, cool, and smelled of lemon dish soap. "Thanks for saving my life. Again."

"Don't mention it."

"Fingers crossed you get your old job back," I whispered. "The post office isn't the same without you."

Her smile was a beautiful reply.

47

THE DRIVE back to my shack along a road I'd recently traveled—bound, gagged, and in the dark—had a surreal feeling to it.

In the aftermath of a near-death experience, as I stared out the window, it was hard to believe I was really here in this moment, sitting beside Keone in his truck, with the yellow-feathered miniature war helmet swinging from the rearview mirror.

"Are you okay?" Mr. K glanced at me, a wrinkle of concern between his brows.

"I feel kind of . . . disconnected." Even my words seemed to hover above my head in an invisible conversation bubble. "I was sure I was going to die. Maybe I haven't got used to being alive instead."

Hana Highway was dark but for the moon overhead, and we'd reached a turn with a shoulder. Mr. K swung the truck off the road abruptly. "I know a place we can talk. There's a fishing spot near here."

"I'm not up for a deep talk and a hike in the dark," I said. "I've done too much of that already tonight."

"I've got nothing like that in mind." He reached across me to the glove box and opened it, fumbling inside for a flashlight. "It's an easy path and I know the way."

"Okay." I owed him that much.

Keone came around to my side of the truck. He opened the door for me. "It's not far. Can I hold your hand?"

I was touched that he remembered to ask permission. "I'm still feeling weird but let's try."

His grip was warm and solid and felt like a magnet holding me in my body as he helped me out of the truck. My feet seemed a long way off, but they followed directions. We pushed through some bushes, following an almost invisible path. "This is a favorite family spot for ulua fishing," Mr. K said. "Those are called giant trevally where you come from."

As we broke free of the overgrowth, I gasped at the view.

We were on a bluff overlooking the ocean. The moon was bright enough that Keone clicked off the flashlight and we were easily able to follow a dirt trail leading down to black lava rocks. Waves broke rhythmically against the stones with a thump-and-shush, as if the planet had a heartbeat.

Keone continued to hold my hand, helping me past rough spots and boulders, and soon we sat on a slab of boulder facing the sea.

In the scope of the panorama before me, my worries and experiences seemed to recede. They were washed away by the churning black water gleaming silver where the waves broke and the arc of moon and stars shone above us.

Keone pointed to a couple of metal tubes sunk into the rocks above the wave line. "Pole holders."

"You said the name of what you're fishing for here? Giant something?"

"Giant trevally. *Ulua*. Good eating. A single fish can feed a family. The smaller ones are easier to catch. They're called *papio*. Jack, on the continent."

"I don't think we have either of those in Maine. Never heard of them."

The easy conversation grounded me further. I was starting to feel more normal, if such a thing was possible in this setting.

"Good fun to sit out here with the bruddahs, down a few beers, talk story after work." Keone lifted his chin, indicating a nearby fire ring. "What the guys do on the weekends."

"Thanks for showing me this. It's helping. I feel better." I squeezed his hand. And then I remembered something I'd been trying hard to forget. "You broke up with me."

My voice choked up on the sentence. I hunched, holding back sobs, and squished my eyes shut to keep tears from squirting out.

"Yeah. About that." Keone squeezed my hand tight, and it felt good. "I overreacted. I'm sorry."

"And I'm sorry I forgot to call you and it was stressful."

"I know you're trying. It's only fair that I try too. I don't want you to be any different, you know." He lifted our hands and pressed them against his chest. I felt the thump of his pulse through our entwined fingers. "Would you be willing to forget that phone call ever happened?"

"Yes, please." I had a big lump in my throat I couldn't speak past.

"Anything else we need to talk about?"

"Nope." I wasn't ready to tell him about my L word revelation. Someday the time would be right.

Keone leaned in to kiss me.

It was a bit damp with tears that must have leaked out somewhere along the way, but sweet for all the salt.

48

ANA:

Seated on the deck of Fabio's yacht, a sunny breeze drying my freshly washed hair, I could almost pretend the events of the previous day and night were a dream.

Or a nightmare.

The skin of my legs itched, and my calves and thighs still ached from the miles we'd run on foot through rugged terrain by the light of our headlamps.

I sat up and reached for a bottle of tanning oil in the holder on the lounge chair. Fabio had given me a fire-engine red bikini whose origin I chose not to question. I liked the way the clingy fabric showed off my figure, and from the way Fabio eyed me from his nearby chaise, he liked it too. I poured Maui Babe coconut tanning oil into my hand and rubbed it on my scratched-up legs. The oil felt soothing.

Once away from Pua and Kat, we'd walked west and toward the coast until we found phone signal. Once his device was working, Fabio had called for the yacht to pick us up at one of the secluded little bays off the coast. The boat had been waiting for us near Kahului, so it had only taken a few hours for our rendezvous.

Dodging the cops had been easy, if a little physically hazardous due to crossing rough wild land in the dark. "Hard to believe everything worked out so well," I mused. "That was a close one."

"We're not safe until we're in international waters," Fabio said. "Don't count your chickens and all that. Money Pit is a fast yacht, but those Coast Guard cutters are faster."

"I'm betting it all on the Money Pit. And you." I leaned over and kissed him quick. "Did I tell you I love the name of this boat?"

"You did." His slow smile was sexy. He held up the radio he'd been using to talk to the captain. "We're almost in international waters, now."

I sat back and untied the straps of the bikini so I wouldn't get tan lines on my shoulders. "I almost feel bad about ditching Mom." I caught Fabio's eye. "They arrested her last night. Charged her with attempted murder for firing her gun. Also assorted misdemeanors like squatting and destruction of property."

"I know. I was the one who told you all that. My contact on the island keeps me informed."

"I guess I'm still amazed we got away. You're so thoughtful, Fabio." I reached for his hand, worried I was being too clingy—but he let me take it, even gave me a squeeze in return. We faced into a blue horizon, the wind soft and clean from off the bow as the yacht plowed along at maximum speed.

The radio beside Fabio burped out an announcement.

"We're in international waters now," Fabio said. "Straight on to Tahiti, a hideout for runaways since the turn of the century."

"I'm looking forward to a new chapter."

"That's exactly what it will be. New passports and fake identities are on their way via a chopper. And now that we're in international waters, the crew is changing us over." Fabio indicated the busy staff, who were dropping the American flag and raising another, new one whose colors I didn't recognize. Another staffer was applying new magnetic signage over the MONEY PIT name on the hull. "We're now a rich couple from Holland honeymooning on our yacht."

"You think of everything." My grin was sappy. I couldn't help it. Fabio Chang was the man of my dreams. "What's the yacht's name now?"

"Cash Cow. In Dutch, of course."

I laughed. "I like that even better."

The radio fizzed out something else. "Roger that," Fabio said. He turned to me. "Chopper with our passports is inbound."

A few minutes later I spotted it. The helicopter was big, black, and sleek, and it moved like an arrow toward us.

Fabio tugged my hand. "Let's go to the top deck where the landing pad is and see what new names they brought us."

"You still haven't even showed me all over this floating palace," I scolded playfully, grabbing my pareo and wrapping myself.

"You needed your rest after we got on board."

"True." I had slept so hard I could barely remember falling into the comfortable bed in his fancy stateroom. I followed Fabio up a steep set of interior stairs, almost a ladder, to the top floor of the yacht.

This area was utilitarian and smaller than the other decks, consisting of a windowed cockpit where the captain and crew operated, and the open helipad.

I hung back in the stairwell as the wind from the rotors and the roar of the engine filled my ears, but Fabio moved forward. I heard voices over the winding down of the blades, and then he called me. "Ana! Come and meet my cousin."

Cousin? Who could that be?

I stifled apprehension and stepped up and out of the narrow stairs, tucking the ends of the pareo around my breasts. I pasted a smile on my face as a man stepped out of the chopper's prop wash to stand beside Fabio.

I disliked him on sight.

Fabio's cousin was of a similar height and build, with short black hair that stirred in the wind and eyes hidden behind shades. He looked a little older than Fabio but had the same feline stylishness my lover did. This guy had power, and he was in charge—I could see it in the way Fabio stood and the tentative way they embraced.

Fabio and the cousin approached me as two more men got out of the chopper close behind, clearly bodyguards.

I took Fabio's arm as they reached me. "Hello. I'm Ana."

"Your reputation precedes you." The cousin had a smile that didn't reach cold dark eyes revealed when he took off the sunglasses. "Terence Chang."

"Pleased to meet you." I held out a hand and was surprised when he kissed it.

"I see why my cousin's fallen so hard for you."

I thought I was past blushing, but my cheeks went hot. Fabio has been talking about me. To his family. That had to mean something.

"I didn't expect you, cuz." Fabio sounded upbeat, nervous. He was never nervous. "It's an honor. Let's go to a private stateroom where we can get out of the wind."

He shook me off and hurried ahead. Terence gestured politely for me to precede him. He followed, and the black-clad goons brought up the rear.

Picking my way down the steep steel steps, I shivered in the breeze off the ocean.

I'd been insulated from Fabio's life as a gangster until now. We were always surrounded by guards and staff at his house and on the yacht. But the gun-toting guards were unobtrusive background décor—servants who made things appear and disappear, there to do our bidding and keep us comfortable and safe.

The men behind me weren't there for my safety, though. I was sure of it.

Terence opened the brass-bound door to the lower deck for me. I took one long, last look at the ocean before I stepped inside the ship. I didn't know when I'd see it again.

49

ONE WEEK LATER:

Opal waved at me from the porch of the general store as I locked up the post office on a Friday afternoon. "Don't forget the party for Edith tonight!"

"Of course not," I hollered back. "TGIF!"

"You mean, '*Pau Hana* Friday.' That's what we say here!"

"That works!" I waved. "See you soon."

I hurried through my closing routine, making sure the pretty lotus-shaped plug-in aromatherapy machine was puffing away in Pua's office—because she was due to return to work on Monday.

I couldn't wait to share the joys, headaches, and responsibilities of the post office with her once more. It would be so nice to have two sets of hands dealing with the village's mail.

Tiki waited for me on the porch of the shack and greeted me by winding around my legs.

I nudged her aside to unlock the door. "Yeah, girl. I'm happy to see you, too." How far we'd come! "I have time for a quick dip in the ocean before I have to get party-ready."

Tiki informed me that she'd prefer her food now, so I obliged, then threw my suit on and ran across the road to jump in.

My phone rang as I was wrapping it in a towel for my swim, and I picked up when I saw my new boss Sophie Smithson's name. "Hey, lady. What's happening?"

"News of Ana and Fabio," Sophie said in her cool Brit accent. I could listen to her talk all day, especially when she was telling me things like this. The turquoise water beckoned, but I parked my buns in the sand for the update.

"What happened with them? I heard the feds thought they'd escaped by boat, since the plane they took out here was ditched in Kahului."

"Yes. I believe that too. Fabio was known to use the Chang family's yacht berthed in Waikiki a lot." She paused. "I don't know if I've told you about my search engine called D.A.V.I.D.—I might as well tell you since you're on my payroll now. It gives us a definite advantage in finding people and information."

"No. What's that?" I massaged my feet through sand still warm from the day's sun.

"Data Analysis Victim Identification Database. DAVID searches the internet for keywords and names, focusing on detecting criminal patterns. It can even dig through classified video for facial recognition patterns. Last week, after Fabio and Ana escaped, I set it to looking for them."

"Wow. I hope the FBI has this program."

"No. A long story, but the main reason why I left the agency. Anyway, I added photos of Ana and Fabio to the search parameters and DAVID found them."

I bounced on the sand. "You're killing me with the long lead-in."

"Well, it's important you understand how I know where they are —because that explains why we can't do anything about it."

"Pua told me Terence Chang was going to 'deal with' them, and he's a gangster, right? You're going to tell me they're in Davy Jones's locker at the bottom of the ocean," I said.

Sophie snorted. "They're alive and well—but working on a coca plantation in Venezuela, which doesn't have extradition to the

U.S. So even if we tip off the FBI, we can't get them back to the states."

"Dangnabbit. I wanted to see that arrogant pair either as shark food or doing time."

"Terence Chang must have decided to keep them alive because Fabio is family. From what I can gather, they're slaves at that coca farm and housed with other workers in a locked bunker. Those two are doing time all right." Sophie's voice was full of satisfaction. "Terence is making them work off the debt they owe from the debacle at New Ohia. I enjoyed snooping on the surveillance footage of them working in the hot sun."

"I'll have to take your word for it."

"Next time we have a case, I'll share the video with you. You deserve to see it, too."

I smiled. "I like the sound of 'next time we have a case.'"

"Oh yes. You're not getting that SUV you call Sharkey for free, you know."

I glanced over my shoulder at where Sharkey was parked in front of the shack. "I'm so glad it's out of the shop."

"And I'm glad you said yes to being my security advisor. I'll be in touch. Have a nice weekend." She ended the call.

I smiled at the phone. "Hard labor in the hot sun of Venezuela as human slaves. I can live with that." I wrapped the phone in the towel, put on my goggles, and hurried to dive into the ocean.

Today was one of the days the green sea turtles, known as *honu* in Hawaiian, swam in to feed on seaweed growing on rocks here and there on the sandy bottom of Ohia Bay. As I did my laps, I watched their smooth gliding movements—they seemed to fly through the water. The *honu* had a lot to teach me about taking things easy and keeping life simple.

Hopefully simplicity would be coming for me, too, as the situation with New Ohia resolved. Though the FBI had been unable to make a case against the Changs, New Ohia Vision, Inc. was shut down and the state had canceled their lease. The assets overseas were being appropriated through a special negotiator. Some of that money would go back to investors, but meanwhile, the grass grew tall, the waterfall was dry, and the lights remained off in New Ohia.

There was talk of the county of Maui appropriating the abandoned development as a park, with the clubhouse and pool being used by the town of Ohia and the model homes being available for county workers, but no one knew anything yet.

I was glad our village would maintain its sweet, slow pace and small-town integrity.

SHOWERED AND CHANGED, my wet hair combed, I was ready for the party. I'd chilled and hulled lychees that I'd bought at Hasegawa's for easy eating, and I filled my one large bowl with them.

Tiki protested my departure as I opened the front door. I pointed over to where Opal and Artie were already sitting on the front porch. "I'll be back soon, girl. Or you can come with me."

Tiki opted to come, padding beside me as I walked over to join my friends in their chairs. Opal had set up all of the extra folding ones for the party. She handed me an ice-cold root beer as I ascended the steps, Tiki at my side.

"We closed early." Opal pointed to a fold-open sign she'd carried over and set up by the road. STORE CLOSED was written on it. A steady stream of cars slowed to read it, then moved on past. Opal adjusted today's purple velour scarf worn with an enormous sparkling peacock pin. She unrolled a hand-painted sign reading WELCOME BACK EDITH on a long roll of butcher paper. "Here, Kat. Help me put this up."

I held one end while Opal wielded a staple gun. We attached the sign across the porch railing. More cars slowed to see if this pertained to them.

"They all want to stop in and join us," I said.

Artie strummed a dramatic chord on his guitar. "*'Ohana* only this evening."

Right on cue, Josie drove up in the VW van bearing Edith, the guest of honor. Clara and Pearl followed in Clara's car, and a few minutes behind, Pua rolled up in her Honda with Sassy riding shotgun.

I hurried over to help Edith out of the van. She wore the same purple caftan I'd last seen Lola wearing, and it gave me a pang to see it. From what I'd heard, Lola was going through a detox program at the jail and doing all right. I breathed a tiny sigh of relief that the Red Hat ladies and I had been able to pool funds and hire a maid service to thoroughly clean Edith's house and do her laundry before she got home. A yard service had cleared up the trash and the lawn and revived her orchids.

My friend was looking good. The pink in her cheeks was echoed by her favorite red hat. I helped her down from the passenger seat. "Did you get settled in at your house okay?"

"I loved Beth and Arnold's place, Fantasia—don't get me wrong, I'm grateful to them—but there's no place like home. I'm so glad to be back," Edith said. "I'm okay to walk by myself, Kat, thank you very much."

Josie came around the front of the van, towing her oxygen tank. "Edie, darling, let Kat help you. For my peace of mind."

The two exchanged a loving glance, then the little lawyer took my arm and leaned on me. It felt good to have her close. "Thanks, Kat. For all you've done to make sure we came to this day."

"You're welcome," I said.

I supported her up onto the porch and helped her get settled beside Artie in the "party throne" as Opal called her usual wooden armchair. A lei of fresh gardenias brought by Pearl was arranged over Edith's shoulders, filling the air with fragrance. She sipped a red cup of fruit punch as everyone stopped by to pay their respects.

Soon a pop-up tent lined with fairy lights was added to the party area. More chairs were dragged from every corner and nearby houses, including mine. The parking lot became crowded when Pono and his family plus the Kaihales from Hana arrived. Villagers like Mrs. Lagustino, Mrs. Vehikite and their families, and even the Nakasones streamed down Hibiscus Street on foot to join the festivities. Everyone brought bowls and platters of food or coolers filled with drinks.

Things really got going when several Kaihale cousins began playing and singing with Artie as Opal organized the potluck buffet on folding tables.

Tiki grew restless with all of the people and darted off the porch, returning to the shack. I made the rounds, "talking story" with everyone—and keeping my eye out for a certain green Toyota truck with surf racks on it.

Another truck arrived—this one an extended cab silver Toyota Tacoma with Stevens behind the wheel and Lei in the front seat. I went over to greet the family and opened the back passenger door for Kiet.

The little boy hopped out, yelling, "Surprise!" That was echoed by Lei and Stevens, and little Rosie clapped her hands. My mouth fell open at the sight of Aunt Fae sitting between Rosie's child seat and Kiet's booster.

"Aunt Fae! What are you doing here?" I exclaimed.

"I had to see you," she said simply. I helped her out as Lei opened the door on the other side to get Rosie.

"I'm so glad you're here!" I pulled Aunt Fae into my arms for a hug. She wore her usual flannel shirt, jeans, and boots even here in the tropics. Iron-gray hair, cut in a sensible shoulder-length bob, caught the last of the sunset, and her deep-set brown eyes were damp as we embraced. Her long body felt light and breakable in my arms. "I can't believe you came all this way. I know you don't like plane flights."

Aunt Fae stood back to get eye contact with me. "I heard from your boss Ben in the Secret Service that he had some concerns about you and the posting out here," she said. "And when I looked online in the news about Hawaii, I saw you were working with Maui Police Department on a case. I called there when I got to the island, and this nice sergeant agreed to bring me out to see you."

"And the timing was perfect to join the party," Lei chimed in, removing a zippered cooler pouch from behind the seats. "You'll get to try my lilikoi meringue pie, Fae."

"It's great that worked out," I agreed. "I still need to pinch myself. I can hardly believe you're here." I pinched my arm in an exaggerated way.

Aunt Fae smiled. "I had to find out what made you turn down an offer to be on the VP's special all-female security team. That would have been your dream job once upon a time."

I'd said no to that opportunity weeks ago. It seemed like old news now. "We're in the middle of a party, Auntie, but I have so much to tell you. Can I introduce you to my friends? And let's get something to eat. You must be starving."

"I could eat," she said. "Lead on, Macduff."

I laughed. I couldn't help it. "You don't know what a kerfuffle that phrase caused with my boyfriend."

"Boyfriend?" Auntie's bushy brows about flew off her forehead in astonishment. "Things are making more sense all of a sudden. Where is he?"

"Keone's not here yet." My face was warm. "Anyway, I misspoke; I'm not sure we're official. I'm still bad at the relationship thing, Auntie. Come meet Edith, the guest of honor."

I was glad of the whirlwind of introductions that came next as I brought my aunt up onto the porch and the Red Hats, including Opal, swamped her as if she were a minor celebrity.

I watched with a grin on my face and wasn't surprised when she went back to the truck to fetch her own red hat out of her duffel bag, a faded canvas bucket-style topper that went great with her flannel shirt. Clara, Edith, Opal, and Pearl applauded.

"We knew there was a reason Kat fit in so well here," Opal said, hugging her. "Turns out it was the woman who raised her."

Since Auntie was occupied, I got into the buffet line for both of us with a couple of sturdy cardboard luau trays. Lei slipped in behind me.

"Sophie tells me you're on her payroll for good," Lei said, hoisting little Rosie onto her hip to keep the toddler out of the serving dishes. "Said you'll be her contact out here for cases."

"I don't know how 'for good' any of this is," I made air quotes on the phrase. "I am on loan from the Secret Service. I have a real job, you know." The thought of returning to Washington, D.C., filled me with existential dread.

"And postmaster isn't a real job?" Stevens's sky-blue eyes teased as he draped a long arm around his wife and daughter. "Plus working for Sophie. We all know what a slavedriver she is."

"We want you to stay. You're good at what you do. You're good for this town," Lei said in her straightforward way. "Plus, I like having a reason to come out to this side of the island. We got a kama'aina special for the night at the Hotel Hana, and we're having a little family getaway."

"I really like what I've got going on here. I just don't know if it's going to last," I said, digging into a pot of rice and then layering on some kalua pork. I filled our trays with a variety of delicious Hawaiian food Auntie would appreciate: *lomilomi* salad, a couple of *laulau*, and a dollop of *poi*. "Looks like someone is having fun," I said, pointing to their son Kiet, running across the road to the beach in the twilight with the Nakasone girls and a pair of flashlights. "Nice to see those girls acting like kids for a change."

Their aunt Lani sashayed up in a short black dress that showed off her figure. "Hey there, Keone," she said to someone behind me. "Long time."

I turned, burdened with the full plates of food. Mr. K had sneaked up, and though he gave Lani a brief nod, his gaze was on mine. He held a lei made of starlike white flowers that emitted glorious fragrance. "Brought you something special," he said. He dropped the lei over my head.

"What's that for?" I smiled at him.

"From my mom." He pointed. Mrs. Kaihale, looking like a queen in a long muumuu, waved from across the porch. "A thank-you for helping save Edith."

"What flowers are these?"

"*Pikake.*"

I found an open spot on a table and set down the cardboard trays. I lifted the strand of flowers to sniff them, closing my eyes. "Unbelievable. It's what angels' sheets would smell like if they had dryer fresheners in heaven."

He snorted a laugh. "You're one of a kind, Kat. Maybe that's why I love you."

I stopped breathing. Did he just say the L word?

"So this is your boyfriend," Aunt Fae said from behind me. "I'm Kat's aunt Fae." She stepped forward, hand extended. "And you are?"

"Keone Kaihale. Kat's boyfriend." He bypassed Auntie's hand in favor of a hug. "Great to meet you. Kat talks about you all the time."

I still hadn't breathed and that caught up with me. I emitted a loud gasp that ended in a cough. I flushed and sputtered as they stared at me.

Keone whacked my back. "We need drinks. I'll get us something." Off he went.

I pointed to the trays. "Let's find a spot to eat."

"With room for three to sit and get acquainted," Aunt Fae said with satisfaction. "I like him."

LATER, when we were dancing in the parking lot to a mellow slack-key song, I rested my cheek on Keone's shoulder. He rested his on mine, our arms looped lightly around each other. All the touching was going fine so far.

"I like how tall you are," I said. "My chin fits right here."

"Same," he murmured.

"When I thought I was going to die, I realized something," I said.

"Must have been important." Mr. K raised his head. His brown eyes were warm and soft in the dim light.

"I saw the people I'd regret never seeing again—the faces of the people I love." I drew a trembling breath, and then said it. "Yours was one of them. I love you, Keone."

"Glad I'm not the only one. I love you, too, Kat," he said, and kissed me.

For once, no one even noticed. We were a small part of something bigger, something wonderful—a village called Ohia, on Maui.

50

ONE MONTH LATER:

I walked beside Aunt Fae through the empty streets of New Ohia on a Friday evening after the post office closed.

The grass had grown since the development reverted to the state. Bushy and green, it engulfed lights that used to shine on artfully planted berms and coconut palms now shaggy with neglect. Those lights contained state-of-the-art deactivated surveillance nodes that had cost a small fortune and now were gathering sowbugs and ants in their crannies.

Meanwhile, without a human presence, wild pigs had moved in from the mountains to tear at the shoulders of the road in search of grubs and tender roots, ripping up the wiring.

"This place has really gone to seed quickly," Auntie commented.

"You'd never know it was fully occupied only a few months ago," I said. "It's the tropics. Everything grows so fast here." I pointed to a family of pigs that hightailed it back into the jungle at the sight of us. "Both flora and fauna."

"Well, that's why they need a caretaker since the place is a state park now." Aunt Fae had legs as long as mine and she kept a pace that caused Tiki, trailing in our wake, to trot to keep up.

"One last time, Auntie—are you sure you want to do this?" We turned into a cul-de-sac that had become familiar to me through multiple impromptu visits.

"Girl, I've never been more certain of anything in my life." Aunt Fae grinned at me. She'd adapted to the climate of Hawaii by trading in her flannel shirts for tank tops, but other than that, her no-nonsense style was unchanged. "I love it here, especially now when winter's got Maine locked down with snow."

Aunt Fae had taken to life in Ohia like a turtle to the sea. She had offered to help Opal and Artie in the store, and soon became an indispensable help to them while I was at work in the post office. She was already fast friends with the Red Hat ladies and loved zipping around the coast visiting and doing errands on the e-bike.

The one sticky bit about her moving to Ohia to live with me was that the shack was awfully small for two, and there were no other available rentals in the area—but that issue had been solved. "I couldn't believe it when Edith stopped by with the state ranger to offer me the job of caretaker at New Ohia and give me this key."

"I wasn't surprised at all. A lot of people have gone out of their way to make sure you want to stay here," Auntie said with satisfaction.

"Well, thank goodness I don't have to keep up the grounds, just oversee things in a general way." I gestured to the junglelike growth around us. "It's not like I need another job. I've got two already."

"We're going to share it. Don't worry." Aunt Fae flexed her skinny bicep. "I may be retired, but I believe in staying busy."

"Good thing. I'm not sure I would have said yes without you on board."

"And needing some space of my own," Auntie said.

"Exactly." We'd made do with an inflatable mattress on the floor of the shack, but both of us were looking forward to having our own bedrooms. "This place should have all the room we need, and more." We approached the model home I'd first got to know by breaking into it looking for evidence after the former tenant had been murdered.

I was apprehensive approaching a house that had been vacated in a hurry by the final manager of the doomed development. The key in my hand felt heavy and hot, as if it carried its own electrical charge. "I don't know what shape it will be inside."

"Don't worry. Whatever they've left it like, we'll roll up our sleeves and make it home. But first, we'll smudge the place and get the bad juju out of there left over from those gangsters. Josie made us a couple of herb bundles for the occasion." Aunt Fae patted the roomy pockets of her cargo pants.

Yep, Auntie fit right in with the quirky characters of our little village, and her sturdy presence at my side was the reassurance I needed to walk up the wide lava stone steps and slide the key into the lock. The bolt turned with a smooth, well-oiled snick, and the gleaming brass handle was easy to press down. I gave the heavy teak door a push and it swung open, revealing an entry lit by a sunbeam from a skylight overhead. I checked the alarm box beside the door; it was off, thankfully.

Tiki padded in from behind me. She walked through the entryway, leading us inside, her kinked tail high and swaying as she inspected the premises. "Good. Moving her here isn't going to be a concern," I said. "Tiki's acting like she owns the place."

Dust motes spun in the sunbeam from overhead, but otherwise the model home was as impersonally clean and staged as it had been designed to be. Terrazzo flooring in a pleasant golden-flecked composite led the eye toward a sunken living room furnished with rattan furniture slipcovered in cream-colored canvas. A few natural fiber area rugs were set off by fake plants that had not suffered from the neglect. The seating arrangement faced a row of glass sliders overlooking a pool hidden by a solar heating cover.

"Wow." Aunt Fae put her hands on her hips. "This is some kind of fancy."

"Yeah." I had a knot in my stomach; it all seemed too good to be true. "The website called the decorating 'beach chic' but fancy is a better word."

"Well." Auntie walked over to the glass coffee table and picked up a squat deity sculpture carved in some kind of stone. "Should we smudge before, or after we see the rooms upstairs?"

"After." I was already missing my humble shack as I poked my head into a huge kitchen gleaming with stainless steel appliances. Nary a gecko poop marred any of the surfaces, though dust had dulled the sheen here and there. "They must have had a pest service as well as a maid service."

"Not anymore," Auntie said. "Don't worry. Your favorite creepy-crawlies will be moving in here in no time. Let's go see the bedrooms."

Tiki opted not to go that far into unknown territory, settling on her haunches in the kitchen to watch for intruders. Auntie led the way up a set of stairs carpeted in an ivory-colored runner that made me worry about tracking in mud.

The second floor consisted of three bedrooms, each with an adjoining bath. Aunt Fae staked a claim on the room with a French door and a little deck that overlooked the driveway, "so I can keep an eye on who's coming and going."

The middle room would make a good guest room/office and was already furnished for that, so I was left with the master bedroom and bath, which took up the back half of the house. Instead of sliders and a deck, the large beach-themed room had a bay window with a comfy-looking lounge seat built over book-shelves. The window overlooked the pool and a view of the jungle and mountains. Evening clouds were tinted salmon with sunset.

I tested the softness of the cotton canvas bench seat with its sand-colored pillows and sighed, longing to curl up there and watch the clouds with a romance novel open on my lap. "I couldn't have designed a more perfect room myself."

Auntie spoke from behind me. "It does look like the pictures you used to collect when you were a little girl. Those book nooks you were so fond of."

"It's so weird this is going to be our place."

"We'll make the most of living here for as long as it lasts," Auntie said with her usual New England practicality. She brandished the bundle of wrapped herbs Josie had given her. "Let's burn that sage now and say a few prayers. Good is going to be happening here, and in Ohia, from now on."

That was my hope, too.

THE NEXT DAY Mr. K arrived with his truck emptied out to help us move from the shack into the house, but in the end, I took very little from the space I'd landed in on my first day in Ohia. The model home was fully furnished all the way down to kitchen utensils so other than re-packing my old suitcase with personal items and clothing, there wasn't much to take.

I gazed around at the simple space holding my favorite cup, the one that read DO NOT SPEAK TO ME UNTIL THIS MUG IS EMPTY. Tweedledum and Tweedledee the geckos were clustered over the stove per usual, with Miss Prissy the cane spider looking on from a corner. The Murphy bed was folded up, the chairs were set under the table, the floor was swept, and the bullet holes were filled.

"This place is ready for the next postal employee," I said, swamped with nostalgia.

Keone rested his chin on my shoulder and put his arms around me; he liked to do that, and I was good with it. "I was thinking the shack would make a good office for a little P.I. firm. K & K Investigations has a ring to it."

I turned and, still holding the mug, draped my arms around his neck. "Are you saying you want to go into business with me? I'm already a private contractor with a security firm."

"That's what I'm saying."

"I thought you didn't like me getting into dangerous situations."

"Maybe I want to be there when you do. Remember when we spied on Lola's phone call? That was fun."

"How could I forget? Your outfit was priceless." We both grinned at the memory of Keone stripping down to his camouflage print boxers for that little adventure.

"I bet we could rent this space for a song. All it really needs is a landline phone and internet," Mr. K said. "Maybe a second desk. The bed could come in handy." He wiggled his brows. "In case we need a nap."

Yeah, things were going very well with the physical side of our relationship, too.

I stepped back to get some breathing room. "This is a big deal. I don't want to start something I can't finish."

"Why? Because you'll be returning to the Secret Service?" He quirked a brow.

"Because I don't want to start something I can't finish," I repeated. "Though yes, it's getting harder to imagine going back to my life in D.C."

I was glad Auntie was already at the new house, putting her things away in her room, so that we could have this discussion—especially when he pulled out a chair and sat, then pushed the other chair away from the table with his foot.

I sat too.

"This could work," he said. "You could contract for Sophie, sure. So could I when needed. My hobby plane might come in handy." He had built a tiny plane that Edith and I had taken to Oahu on an unforgettable flight that I didn't care to repeat anytime soon. "Investigation could be a good side gig. We could do small jobs. Find missing pets and runaway kids. Do background for Edith's legal cases. Not everything has to be a major crime investigation."

"And I hope it wouldn't be." I tapped my lips with a forefinger, my gaze on Tweedledee, positioned to make a run at a moth fluttering around the bulb over the stove. I'd learned to tell them apart since Tweedledee lost its tail to Tiki, narrowly escaping a brush with death. "I would need to resign from the Secret Service if we went forward with this."

He said nothing, too smart to push me in any way.

I leaned back in the chair and shut my eyes, trying to imagine saying goodbye to my friends in this little village. Each person's face as it came to my mind's eye brought a little 'ping' of affection, joy, annoyance, laughter, or love.

Tiki dug her claws into my jeans and climbed up my leg into my lap, purring like a motorcycle without a muffler. The twenty-pound love kitten sat on my stomach demanding head rubs, which I happily gave her.

Could I exchange the 'ohana I had found here (which included Tiki and swimming with turtles on a regular basis) for the rubber chicken dinners and intermittent danger and boredom that had made up the days of my former life?

I had known the answer for a while now but needed a reason to pull the trigger. "I'll call Ben and put in my notice. Then we can talk turkey about K & K Investigations."

Keone swept me into his lap, displacing Tiki, and kissed me soundly. The man had excellent nonverbal skills, and mine were getting better with ongoing practice. I hoped that would continue indefinitely into the future—but as Aunt Fae said, I'd enjoy it as long as it lasted.

ACKNOWLEDGMENTS

Aloha dear readers!

Thanks so much for going on another fun adventure with Kat and her cohort of friends, family, and feline in the wonderful imaginary town of Ohia on Maui.

Hawaii Time is the final book in a planned trilogy, and I hope you enjoyed reading as much as I enjoyed writing this expansion of the Paradise Crime World. That world now consists of the Paradise Crime Mysteries (with Lei) the Paradise Crime Thrillers (with Sophie) and now, the Paradise Crime Cozy Mysteries with Kat! It's a delight to build an interrelated series that meshes characters with genres.

I have been keeping a close eye on the numbers, and the number of fans of the cozies have now equaled those of a Lei or Sophie book, which is good news! That means I have another series I can periodically add a story to. Having the different genres and storylines keeps my interest going, and I hope it does for you too.

If you want to keep reading in the Paradise World, I have lots more for you, beginning with FREE books Blood Orchids and Wired Rogue. If you liked those and still want another FREE book, sign up for my newsletter HERE and get a copy of Torch Ginger, Book 2 in Lei's series.

One last favor—if you liked the story, please take a moment to add a review of Hawaii Time on any retailer or my website. It only takes a few minutes, and it helps more than you know!

Until next time, I'll be writing.

Much aloha,

Toby Neal

P.S. Keep in touch and get a free book (or two!) http://tobyneal.net/TNNews

ABOUT THE AUTHOR

Kirkus Reviews calls Neal's writing, "persistently riveting. Masterly."

Readers rave: "We love Toby's fast-paced, character-driven stories set in the paradise world of Hawaii. Nobody can read just one!"

Award-winning, USA Today bestselling social worker turned author Toby Neal grew up on the island of Kauai in Hawaii. Neal is a mental health therapist, a career that has informed the depth and complexity of the characters in her stories.

You can get TWO FREE award-winning, full-length books by signing up for her email newsletter!

http://tobyneal.net/TNNews

Made in the USA
Middletown, DE
05 February 2024

48597528R00158